From They Rang Up the Police

Detective-Inspector Guy Northeast, of the C.I.D., sat in a third-class carriage and gazed sullenly through the window, which the elderly lady opposite had asked him to close. He had passed through the emulous little heaths of Surrey into the pleasant farmlands of Hampshire and corn was ripening and bullocks fattening, but neither the beauties of nature nor the prospect of a satisfactory harvest could brighten his mood of black despondency. He was crying for the moon. Like many another he was asking to be given back an hour, which had long since passed into that exasperating unimaginable nowhere where the flame of the candle goes—the hour between nine and ten of that blasted Monday morning, when with heaven knows what ideas in his silly young head he had dashed out of Aunt Millie's house in Raynes Park, where he had been stopping over the weekend, and had traveled, hurrying from tram to bus and from bus to underground, to enlist in the Metropolitan Police Force.

Now he was traveling through Hampshire to investigate the disappearance of a spinster of uncertain age, who was obviously suffering from sex repression. "Nothing much in this, Northeast," Superintendent Hannay had said. "Of course, the bag turning up at Waterloo may indicate that she is in London; otherwise there's nothing that Melchester couldn't handle. However, the Chief Constable down there seems to be a friend of the family and he's been pulling strings here—got a wife who's got a brother who's got a wife who's got a husband. You'd better take the bag down and get it identified and look round a bit. I expect you'll get a pretty frigid reception from the blokes at Melchester."

Mysteries by Joanna Cannan

Featuring Inspector Ronald Price
Murder Included (1950)
In the U.S.: *Poisonous Relations*
and *The Taste of Murder*
Body in the Beck (1952)
Long Shadows (1955)
And Be a Villain (1958)
All Is Discovered (1962)

Featuring Inspector Guy Northeast
(both published by The Rue Morgue Press)
They Rang Up the Police (1939)
Death at The Dog (1941)

THEY RANG UP
THE POLICE

by

JOANNA CANNAN

The Rue Morgue Press
Boulder, Colorado

FIRST AMERICAN EDITION

New material © 1999 by
The Rue Morgue Press

0-915230-27-5

The Rue Morgue Press
P.O. Box 4119
Boulder, Colorado 80306

PRINTED IN THE UNITED STATES OF AMERICA

The cover illustration is by Helen Allingham and first
appeared in 1909 in *The Cottage Homes of England*.

Introduction

Young Inspector Guy Northeast makes his debut in *They Rang Up the Police*, the author's first detective novel, published in England in 1939 and one of only two books in which he was to appear. Northeast arrives at Marley Grange and "its household of unhappy women," as he was to refer to it later, not long after he had followed up his promotion to Detective Inspector, C.I.D., with a disastrous performance on a case. As a consequence he is enduring a series of dull, routine assignments, here being packed off to Melchester to investigate the disappearance of a middle-aged spinster from her home.

Northeast, the third son of a Wiltshire farmer, is a big, raw-boned man whose youth, slowness of speech and lack of formal education belie his very real gift for police work. Never in *They Rang Up the Police* is he given any credit, either by his colleagues or the local citizenry, for his part in solving the crime. Northeast's character, tentatively sketched in here, is more fully delineated in *Death at The Dog* (1941), in which the lady novelist Crescy Hardwick helps define him to the reader, explaining that "Education's all very well for dining-out on, but it can't make fools wise. A wise lad, Northeast, and wisdom is common sense lit by imagination."

Even given his short career, Guy Northeast is one of the more interesting detectives to grace the pages of an English Golden Age mystery novel. It was a period when aristocratic amateurs (Dorothy L. Sayers' Lord Peter Wimsey and Margery Allingham's Albert Campion), Oxbridge-educated gentleman coppers (Ngaio Marsh's Roderick Alleyn and Michael Innes' John Appleby), and brilliant scientists (R. Austin Freeman's Dr. John Thorndyke and John Rhodes' Dr. Priestley) dominated the pages of detective novels. (And then there was the odd little foreigner such as Christie's Hercule Poirot or the busybody spinster such as Miss Marple or Patricia Wentworth's Miss Silver.)

Guy Northeast, however, rose to his position in the police from the ranks of Britain's yeoman class, the class that carried the British flag to every corner of the Empire but usually made its appearance in crime fiction only in the role of the long-suffering or blundering second banana to the Great Detective. Northeast is certainly a breath of fresh air in a genre dominated by "nobs."

Britain may have been a democracy in the 1930s, but it was far from a classless society, and the Bolshevik threat was on the minds of many upper-crust Brits. Working-class Bolshies like Funge, the chauffeur in *They Rang Up the Police*, are a common fixture in the crime fiction of the day and are usually portrayed in an unfavorable light, an affectation that almost fatally marred Ngaio Marsh's 1934 debut, *A Man Lay Dead*. Cannan presents a much more balanced view. While the monied class heaps scorn on Funge and is more than willing to assign him the role of a murderer, the Cathcarts' cook remarks that his type often make the best husbands. Although Cannan herself was born into the English intelligentsia, she pokes fun at snobbish high-ranking coppers who refuse to consider that anyone to the manor born could possibly resort to anything as common as murder. Northeast may have little use for higher-ups in the Melchester police, but the lessons of a lifetime are not easily put aside and he, too, occasionally falls into the trap of assigning too much importance to class.

Northeast also differs from most other fictional detectives of the time in his understanding of how close any of us might come to the scaffold, given the opportunity and the means. He's come a long way from the 16-year-old farm boy who dreamed of tracking down thieves and killers as a Royal Canadian Mounted Policeman.

Northeast is a complicated character, filled with longings and regrets and saddled with unvoiced ambitions, and it is his personality that lifts *They Rang Up the Police* above most of its contemporaries. This first mystery lacks the tension created by the interplay between Northeast and his chief suspect, Crescy Hardwick, in its successor, *Death at The Dog*, a book that prompted the *Times* of London to compare newcomer Cannan most favorably to her more established contemporaries: "It is perhaps not entirely to the credit of regular writers of this type of fiction that by reason of her skilled writing and brilliant characterization she should at once beat most of them at their own game."

But if *They Rang Up the Police* doesn't quite match the standard set in *Death at The Dog*, it is still a very fine example of the detective fiction of its time, as well-plotted as a Christie but with perhaps a more balanced and realized world view. Although she employs many of the now timeworn conventions of the period, Cannan isn't content to treat the detective story as a mere game and has one her characters remark: "The bother about detective stories is that they're not in the least like life. People find a body and make no more fuss than if it was a dead rabbit."

Both Northeast books are set in a fictionalized version of rural Oxfordshire, called Loamshire in *Death at The Dog*, published two years later, but never named in *They Rang Up the Police*, although the action takes place in the same towns and villages and Northeast works with the same local police, the obstinate Superintendent Dawes and the blustering Chief Constable, Major Carruthers. The Dog, the pub in which the squire is murdered in the second book, is nowhere to be found in *They Rang Up the Police*, although another pub, the Dog and the Duck, is prominently featured. In both books Northeast is put up at the Red Lion in Melchester, a cheerless establishment with uninviting rooms and indigestible meals, the memory of which stays with him for years to come.

After *Death at The Dog*, Cannan deserted detective fiction for nine years. When she finally did take up the genre again it was with a new character, Inspector Ronald Price, who was introduced to the reading public in 1950 in her most famous novel, the frequently reprinted and retitled *Murder Included*, first published in the United States as *Poisonous Relations* and twice later reprinted as *The Taste of Murder*.

Cannan's daughter Josephine Pullein-Thompson, herself the author of three crime novels, said her mother dropped Northeast as her sleuth "because he was too nice. She much preferred her hate relationship with the awful Price," possibly because "it was too difficult to write about good or nice people." That may be, but Northeast is too complex a character ever to become boring, and the final scene in *Death at The Dog* will tear at the hearts of all but the most hardened readers. Perhaps Cannan felt that Northeast deserved a little peace.

"Awful" is a good description for Price, who foreshadows the equally loathsome sleuths Jack Rosher and Inspector Dover, respectively created many years later by Jack S. Scott and Joyce Porter. Critics Jacques Barzun and Wendell Hertig Taylor, in their highly opinionated *A Catalogue of Crime*, praise Cannan's work but admit that "Price is a caricature" whose "genteel-vulgar traits, speech, and habits" are "deliberately overdone in order to permit a hostile kind of humor at his expense." In spite of the success of the first Price book, the other four in the series have never been commercially reprinted in the United States (an edition of *The Body in the Beck* designed for libraries was published in 1983).

The locale in *They Rang Up the Police* and *Death at The Dog* is a thinly disguised version of rural Oxfordshire, where Joanna Cannan settled with her husband and four children in 1932. "The Dog" is based on a real pub, The New Inn at Kidmore End, which is still in operation and lies near Reading. During the war, especially, the pub was the center of village social life, and Cannan and her family spent many an evening there.

Before she tried her hand at detective fiction, Cannan's books dealt primarily with the aftermath of World War I and life in England during the Great Depression, although several of her novels did have elements of crime fiction in them. All show her keen interest in the social mores of the day and how people behave in difficult times.

During the war, Cannan devoted her energies with great success to writing fiction for young readers. According to daughter Josephine, her mother's "pony" books changed the horse book genre. "Pre-Cannan the central character had always been the horse or pony," Josephine said. "She introduced the first human heroine, a pony fanatic called Jean." Altogether Cannan published nine books for children between 1936 and 1957. She died in 1961 after a long bout with tuberculosis.

Born in Oxford in 1898, Cannan came to the literary life quite naturally. Gilbert Cannan, the novelist who ran off with Mrs. Barrie, was Joanna's cousin, and her father Charles was an Oxford don and Dean of Trinity who became Secretary to the Delegates of the Oxford University Press. Many of Charles Cannan's friends were poets and publishers who made frequent visits to his home.

Joanna's sisters also embraced the literary life. Dorothea married John Johnson, printer to the Oxford University Press, but didn't write herself, while another sister, May Wederburn Cannan, was a noted World War I poet who was engaged to Bevil Quiller Couch, son of Q., who, having barely survived the fighting, died of the black flu shortly after the armistice. With her sisters (to whom she gave most of the credit) Joanna helped edit at the age of ten *The Tripled Crown: A Book of English, Scotch and Irish Verse for the Age of Six to*

Sixteen.

All four of her own children became writers. In addition to her crime fiction, Josephine Pullein-Thompson has written numerous books for older children while Christine, the most prolific, has written for a younger age group. In addition to books for children, Diana also wrote a biography of Gilbert Cannan and two other books for adults. Like their mother and aunts, Josephine and her twin sisters collaborated as teenagers during the war on a book for children. Publication was held up until 1946 due to paper shortages. Joanna's only son, Denis, is a playwright whose first play was performed at the Citizens Theatre in Glasgow after he returned from the war. His second play was directed by Laurence Olivier and was a West End success and went on to New York. Joanna Cannan would no doubt be pleased that her children continue to carry on the family's long-time love affair with words.

Why Joanna Cannan's mysteries haven't been more successful in the United States is something of a mystery itself. Perhaps it's because Northeast was too realistic a character for a time when readers were looking for distractions from the war, while the unlikable Price might have been a hard sell for an American audience used to sophisticated and well-mannered British sleuths. That was unfortunate. Cannan's books deserve a place on the bookshelves alongside the works of Tey, Allingham, Sayers, Marsh, Brand and Heyer. She's that good.

This is the first American edition of *They Rang Up the Police,* which, like several of the Inspector Price mysteries, was never published outside of England and consequently has been extraordinarily difficult to find on the antiquarian market. We hope the present volume and its successor, *Death at The Dog* (also available from the Rue Morgue Press), will help to introduce modern readers to this very talented and much under-appreciated practitioner of the literate English village mystery.

Tom & Enid Schantz
July 1999
Boulder, Colorado

FRIDAY

"SHALL I TURN on the wireless, darling?"

"Not on my account," said Mrs. Cathcart. "This book is quite interesting."

"Is it the one I chose?" asked Delia.

"Yes, darling. It was very clever of you to pick such a nice murder. The last one the girl recommended was so dry that I had to skip most of it."

"The bother about detective stories is that they're not the least like life. People find a corpse and make no more fuss than if it was a dead rabbit," said Delia.

"I know. I can't think how some of these writers get their tales printed."

"I expect," said Delia, who was the most worldly of the Cathcarts, "that they have friends who are printers."

"Or publishers," said the more highbrow Sheila.

"But," said Mrs. Cathcart, "if any of you girls would like the wireless . . . ?"

Delia said, "You, Sheila?"

"No, darling. It's only jazz. But perhaps Nancy . . . ?"

"I don't think there's anything I want to hear," said Nancy. "'But if anyone else . . . ?"

"I heard the tennis results," said Delia, "before dinner. There seems to have been quite an incident during one of the matches. One of the players made a frightful fuss about this, that and the other. Very unsporting!"

Neither Sheila nor Nancy was interested in sport and, though

11

Nancy was only sewing and Sheila staring into space, it almost seemed as if Delia's remark would provoke no comment. But, as Mrs. Cathcart used to explain to admirers of the harmonious daily life of this household of women, it's illogical, it's unintelligent to cast off your good manners just where they are most needed. Perhaps she was old-fashioned: at Marley Court the Ladies Patricia and Angela bickered incessantly; Marley Rectory was a bear garden: but she had brought up *her* girls to be as courteous and considerate to each other as they were to strangers, and now, engrossed as she was, she lifted her wispy gray head and agreed with Delia: "Dreadfully unsporting!"

Sheila, who had been lying back in the big armchair, sat suddenly forward.

"Oh, but darling, don't you think there was some excuse for her? She must have been all wrought up." Sheila's pale eyes blinked behind her thick-lensed glasses. "Like an artist."

"An artist," echoed Delia, but with scorn in the place of Sheila's breathless reverence. "I suppose your idea is that a player who wins a championship automatically develops an artistic temperament. But I don't believe there is such a thing as an artistic temperament. It's not temperament, darling; it's temper."

"Yes," said Sheila, "it may be." She blinked rapidly and brought out, "But in an artist one excuses temper."

"But why, darling?"

"Oh," said Sheila, shy of explaining herself; "oh, because artists aren't like other people. I don't mean that they're superior, darling. As human beings they're definitely inferior, I'm sure. *I was a reed and the wind blew through me. . . .*"

Nancy looked up from her sewing. Delia hadn't changed for dinner; she had been schooling a young horse in the paddock until it had been time to listen to the Wimbledon results, and then it had been dinner time; and she was wearing jodhpurs, a shirt and a horsey tie. But Mrs. Cathcart had changed into a loose coat of purple velvet, a black satin skirt and a necklace of uncut amethysts, and Sheila and Nancy wore silk afternoon dresses, their "garden party frocks" of the year before. Sheila's dress was green. She liked to wear greens and browns, partly because greens and browns made her think of beech woods and beech woods made her think of music, and partly out of consideration for her one beauty—her flaming auburn hair. Nancy's dress was of bright flowered silk, to the casual eye indistinguishable from the material which she was sewing. Nancy was pale and of an angelic fairness; she was small-boned and shorter than either of her sisters; had she chosen dark colors and heavy materials, her fairness and fragility would have been striking: as it was, she looked faded. She was thirty-eight—five years younger than Delia—but, though Delia's solid face was lined and weather-beaten, you didn't think, looking at her, how time passes and where's Helen, where's Thais? You thought that when you looked at Nancy and then, if you were old and had done most things, or young and meant to do everything, you cracked a joke at the expense of "the Cathcart girls."

Nancy opened her mouth to say something, but at the same time Delia began to speak, and her voice was the louder. She said, "Well, darling, we're none of us artists, so we needn't argue. But I must say I shouldn't mind being a reed and the wind blowing through me on a night like this."

She rose a little stiffly and walked to the window pushing back the serviceable hairnet, which kept her brown head neat and masculine, so that it left a hot red line across her forehead. Marley Grange is sheltered from the Melchester road by laurels and conifers, and in the drawing room only the bay window at the east end commands a view. You look across the tennis lawn and the paddock, where Delia's bay hunter, Skylark, was eating his head off, to the wide open pasture which rises to Marley Clump, five tall beeches standing in a confidential circle, lily-green in spring time, secret-green in summer, sun-gold in October, and in winter, stripped of their disguises, gray as wizards' spells. The round midsummer moon was rising now above the beeches; baby rabbits boxed and scuttered across the darkening pasture; a man and a girl emerged from the shadow of the Clump and loitered down the chalky thread that led diagonally across the hill.

Delia began to talk about her horses. "I must say I was worrying over this dry weather; there's scarcely any grass. But it doesn't seem to matter to Skylark. The old wretch is as fat as a pig. By the way, I wish you dear people would lay off feeding sugar knobs to Flavia. I want her to realize that sugar comes as a reward when she's done something properly. I can't do that if she's getting it every time any of you pass the stable." Delia was good to her horses, but she didn't spoil them or sentimentalize over them. She fed them well, worked them hard, petted them if they behaved and beat them if they didn't, and when they got too old and slow for her, she advertised them scornfully for sale as suitable mounts for nervous ladies or elderly men.

Neither Sheila nor Nancy rode now. Sheila had never cared for

it and Nancy had lost her nerve after numerous falls from half-bro-
ken ponies, whose antics Delia enjoyed. But both were fond of horses,
and liked petting them, while Mrs. Cathcart pitied them as she pitied
all animals, dumb things that couldn't tell you what was the matter
with them, soulless things without morals or the hope of a heavenly
crown. For seventy years Grace Cathcart had lived the insane life of
human beings, but never had it occurred to her that the thicket which
words are, a license to love, a soul to tremble for, would be a poor
exchange for joy in the morning, sex absolved, thanks at evening
and death in faith.

She said, "I'm afraid I must plead guilty, darling. But I can't
resist Flavia. Such a wistful face!"

"She puts that on," said Delia. "Seriously, darling. . ."

"Very well, darling," said Mrs. Cathcart. "I'll harden my heart."
She returned to her book, congratulating herself on this easy little
example of give and take.

Delia didn't care for reading or sewing: she was fond of bridge,
but her mother and sisters played atrociously; Patience bored her,
so there was nothing to do but to stand at the window, thinking of
her horses, thought Mrs. Cathcart, looking up now and then, still the
anxious mother. And Sheila's thinking of her music, she thought,
and Nancy of the pretty, fresh little frock she's making; and, she
thought, how well we fit in, Delia, the man of the family, Sheila, the
highbrow, and Nancy our home bird. I'm lucky to have my darlings
still with me, she thought; after all, marriage isn't everything; and
she remembered how Humphrey had snored, what dirt he'd brought
in on his shooting boots, *that* Mrs. Featherstone, the eternal trouble
over the kedgeree. No, marriage isn't all beer and skittles. . . . She
read on.

Delia said, "I do believe that's Jessie coming down from the
Clump with Albert Funge."

Mrs. Cathcart said, "Well, darling, what am I to do? I spoke to
her. I told her that she was far too young to be thinking of boys, and
I warned her that next time she was late in, she would have to go."

Delia looked at her wristwatch.

"It's ten minutes to ten."

"Then she'll be in in time," said Sheila.

"She won't," said Delia. " If she came straight in she would, but I
bet you anything she'll spend hours saying good night to that disgusting youth in Lovers' Lane."

"Oh dear," said Mrs. Cathcart, "and it's so hard to get them now."

"She won't be much loss," said Delia. "She's a revolting little creature, anyway."

"But, darling, she's quite obliging," said Sheila. "She can dust a room without disturbing everything, and she washes stockings well."

"It is her," confirmed Delia, now that the entwined figures had come nearer. "She's got on that orange frock of Nancy's that stretched so. I must say, Nancy, it looks better without that awful rust-colored belt you would wear with it, but I shouldn't have thought you would have given it to her. She hasn't been with us long, and it would have done for Mrs. Groves."

Nancy said nothing. Mrs. Cathcart said, "I expect our baby only wanted to be kind. And perhaps Jessie won't be late after all. I do hope she won't. I don't want unpleasantness and all the bother of getting a new between-maid."

"Well," said Delia, "I shall lock up as usual at ten. If she's still out, she'll have to knock. And don't you do anything, darling. If I've gone to bed, I'll hear her from the lawn."

"Are you going to sleep out again, darling?"

"Yes, darling. It's lovely. I can't think why the others don't."

"It's so noisy, darling," said Sheila. "Skylark scrunches all night and things rustle."

"I don't hear anything," said Delia. "As soon as my head touches the pillow, I'm fast asleep. But I should have thought that even scrunching and rustling were preferable to the stuffiness of the house on a night like this."

Nancy was folding up her sewing. "I think I'll go to bed now," she said.

"Is our baby tired?" asked Mrs. Cathcart tenderly.

"I am rather," said Nancy. "I didn't sleep very well last night."

"You do look rather washed out, darling," said Delia. "You should take more exercise. I go fast asleep as soon as my head touches the pillow. You can't expect to sleep well if you sit indoors all day sewing."

"But not many girls," said Mrs. Cathcart, "are as strong as you are, Delia. I remember old Doctor Stenning saying that he had never seen a finer girl baby."

"Now, darling, don't start remembering," said Delia. "It's your bedtime, too. And if you finish that book tonight, you'll have nothing to read tomorrow."

"I've just got to the murder," said Mrs. Cathcart. "I'm sure I know who did it." But she shut up her book and rose. "Coming,

Sheila?"

"Oh . . . oh yes," said Sheila and scrambled to her feet and stood blinking, a tall, ungainly figure.

"I'll let out John," said Delia.

"No, darling, I'll do it," said Sheila.

"I'll let him out," said Nancy.

"No, darling. You're tired. You run off to bed-byes," said Delia.

Hearing his name spoken, John, the stout liver spaniel, climbed from his basket and stood beaming at his slaves. The three women dashed to the door. It was delightful, their mother thought, to see them so eager to outdo one another in unselfishness.

Delia's and Nancy's hands met on the doorknob.

"I can get my bed ready while I'm waiting for him," said Delia. "You see Mother upstairs."

Nancy slowly drew back from the door. "Come along, old man," said Delia, and John waddled after her into the hall.

Mrs. Cathcart was shaking up the cushions—pink cushions, which, lying in armchairs and sofas covered with mauve and blue cretonne, gave an effect of sweet-pea coloring in harmony with the bright, calm atmosphere of Marley Grange. Shaking and smoothing, she thought: such a pretty restful room . . . so much easier without a man in the house—no pipes, no greasy head, no loud, complaining voice, a smell of flowers instead of that disagreeable smell of perspiration and tobacco. I've nothing to reproach myself with, she thought. I was a good, faithful wife to dear Humphrey; he's at rest now, and oh, the peace of it, she thought, seeing in anticipation her bedroom upstairs, the rose-colored single bed, the glass of boiled milk on the night table, Nancy, Sheila, Delia saying, "Good night, darling; sleep well," and closing the door softly behind them. And then—no stamping in the dressing room, no snores, no clearing of a smoker's throat, no arguments about the number of blankets, no sounds, no movement, no will but her own.

"Ready, darling?"

"Yes, darling."

Nancy held the door open and, with a hand under her mother's elbow, piloted her upstairs.

"Bottle hot?" said Nancy, feeling the mound in the bed; and, "Milk?" she said, looking on the night table; and, "A fresh supply of biscuits," she announced, looking in the biscuit tin covered with purple satin and ornamented with a pink silk rose. "Everything seems all right, darling."

"Thank you, my pet," said Mrs. Cathcart, raising her stiff old arms to undo the clasp of her necklace. "I don't know what I should do without my girls. There aren't many modern young people who would bother about a poor, ugly old woman."

"Now, darling, if you're going to be morbid . . . ."

"I'm not morbid, darling. I'm only grateful for all your loving kindness. In these days happy homes like ours are few and far between—at least so everybody tells me. Oh dear, these tiresome little hooks. . . . Could you, darling?"

Nancy unhooked the little net modesty vest and kissed her mother. "Good night. Sweet dreams. And don't be too long, dear—I'll turn your bath on."

"Thank you, darling."

Nancy shut the door softly behind her and walked down the passage to the bathroom. Marley Grange only possessed one bathroom, and this was a disadvantage when the Cathcarts were going to Southwold for their summer holiday and wanted to let the house. Prospective tenants always demanded two bathrooms, which was absurd, the Cathcarts thought, because, with a little organization and thought for others, they managed perfectly with one.

As Nancy went into the bathroom and Sheila, tunefully whistling an air from *Figaro*, came upstairs, the hall clock struck ten. Delia was dragging her camp bed from the verandah, where it was placed in the daytime, made up ready for her, but discreetly covered by a paisley shawl. She heard the church clock strike and, as soon as she had placed her bed in the position she liked, she called to John and took him into the house through the front door. Marley Grange can be said to face east, because the big drawing-room window and the dining-room windows face that way; but the front door is in the north side of the house and the lawn, where Delia slept, lies between the west wall of the drawing room and the drive. Delia had chosen this sleeping place on account of the seclusion offered by the tall yew hedges on three sides of the lawn. To reach the front door, she passed through a wicket gate at the north end of the verandah, and, at the sound of her footsteps crunching on the gravel sweep, the young mare, Flavia, whinnied. Delia answered her with a kindly, "Good night, little girl."

John slept in the lobby. Although, theoretically, he was Nancy's dog, he had been well-trained by Delia and he knew his routine. He clambered into his basket, curled up and firmly closed his eyes. Delia passed through the hall and turned into the passage which led to the kitchen quarters. With the lamentable exception of Jessie, the maids had gone to bed, and they had left the kitchen in a state that Delia would have to speak about—crumbs and cheese-rind on the table, dirty cups containing . . . yes, cocoa, in the scullery sink, too much coal for either safety or economy on the fire. Delia took the top off the fire, found the tongs, which had been carelessly thrown under the fender, picked out the lumps of coal and piled them on the range to cool. Then she raked out the ashes with what she perceived to be the poker from the spare bedroom.

It was a quarter past ten by the kitchen clock when Delia had finished tidying up after the maids. Jessie wasn't in and Delia didn't intend to listen to any excuses; on a still night like this you couldn't miss hearing the church clock from Marley Clump, much less in Lovers' Lane. Delia switched off the kitchen light, walked to the end of the passage and resolutely turned the key in the back door.

Then she shot the bolts. One and then another went sharply home. From the other side of the door came a muffled exclamation and the sound of scurrying feet. Jessie tried the handle, rattled it, then knocked—for obvious reasons, thought Delia, ignoring the electric bell.

Delia let Jessie knock. After a moment or two, she heard a creak on the back stairs. She looked up. Elspeth, the housemaid, was peering over the banisters, In a pink flannel dressing gown and long fair plaits, she looked odd, thought Delia . . . not like a maid.

"What do you want, Elspeth?"

"Someone's knocking, Miss."

"I know," said Delia. "It's Jessie. She's late again. You can go to bed, Elspeth. I'll let her in."

Elspeth vanished. Delia waited till she was back in her bedroom and then she opened the door.

Jessie said, "Oh!"

Delia said, "I'd like to know what you mean, Jessie, by not being in on time?"

"Oh," said Jessie, "I didn't know as I wasn't. The church clock has only just gone ten."

"I heard the church clock," said Delia. "It struck ten at least twenty minutes ago."

"Well, I'm sorry, Miss," said Jessie. "I 'eard it go as I stood by the gate and then I just said good-bye to my friend."

"It's no use making excuses," said Delia. "You know perfectly well that you're supposed to be in by ten. Mrs. Cathcart spoke to you

last week, and she warned you that if you were late again you'd have
to go. This is flagrant disobedience, and we could dismiss you without notice if we chose."

"Oh, Miss, you aren't going to give me my notice?"

"Yes, I am," said Delia. "You can stay till we're suited," she added
prudently, "but as soon as we've found another girl, you can go."

"Oh, Miss, please. . ."

A man stepped briskly from the laurels.

"There's no 'please, Miss,' about it. Don't you lower yourself,
Jess. This ain't the only 'ouse in the neighbor'ood, and a girl like you
don't want to be working for a lot of fussy old maids."

"Funge!" said Delia.

"Yes, Miss?" said Albert readily.

"How dare you speak like that?"

"Oh, I dare all right," said Albert. "I'm not afraid of you. Well
off you may be, but you're only biscuits when all's said and done."

"Jessie," said Delia, "you'd better come indoors. Funge, I shall
speak to Mr. Hislop about you tomorrow."

"Speak away," said Albert. "What I does out of working hours is
no concern of 'Islop's, and you know that as well as I do."

"We'll see about that," threatened Delia.

"Yes," said Albert, "we will. And I 'ope it's understood that Jessie
leaves 'ere at 'er month and no waiting till you're suited with another girl. And if you wants another girl, Miss Cathcart, I'd advise
you to look beyond the village, where they don't know you so well. A
parcel of old cats like you don't know 'ow to treat a girl. Can't get
'usbands yourselves, so you don't want no one else to. That's what
'tis. So long, Jess," said Albert and strode away.

"Well!" gasped Delia, and then, "Really, Jessie, I can't think how
you can have taken up with such a horrible, impertinent young man."

"Oh well, Miss," said Jessie, "there's two sides to every question,
isn't there?"

Delia looked down at her. She was a short, plump girl with bright
brown eyes, round red cheeks and straight, cropped brown hair:
like a robin, Sheila had said, when Jessie first came, and seemed
satisfactory; like a cheeky sparrow, Delia thought now.

"You'd better go to bed before you say any more, Jessie. If you
think you can be as rude as you like because you're going, you'd
better think again. You'll have to get a reference from Mrs. Cathcart
wherever you go."

Jessie turned away. "Good night, Miss Delia," she said cheerfully and ran upstairs.

Conscious of an unaccustomed sense of defeat, Delia locked and bolted the door. Then she walked down the passage and upstairs to her mother's room. Mrs. Cathcart was in bed sipping her milk. She said, "Oh, there you are, darling. I heard voices. Was it you talking to that girl?"

"Yes, darling. She tried to make excuses, but I wasn't taking any, and then that poisonous Albert Funge appeared and chipped in. He was awfully rude. I gave Jessie notice and I told Albert I would speak to Mr. Hislop about him."

"It's all settled then?"

"Yes, except for speaking to Mr. Hislop. I'll do that, darling."

"Thank you, Delia. I'm sorry you had all that unpleasantness. What did Funge say?"

"Oh, he was just rude. I don't mind the unpleasantness."

"I do envy you your strong character," said Mrs. Cathcart admiringly. "I don't know what we should do without you—the man of the family, I always say."

Delia laughed. "Well, Sheila's always in the clouds and Nancy's such a gentle little thing. Some one must cope. . . . Finished your milk, darling? Well, good night, darling. Shall I turn off the light?"

"Yes, please. Good night, darling. Sweet dreams."

Delia kissed her mother, turned off the light and shut the door. She could hear Sheila whistling in the bathroom, so she called out, "Good night," and Sheila answered, "Good night, D. Sleep well." Nancy, who, like Delia, had her bath in the mornings, was already in bed, and she murmured, "Good night," very sleepily when Delia peeped round her door. "Such a tired little girl," said Delia tenderly, and passed on into her own room.

Delia's room was mannish. The furniture was solid mahogany; the carpet was brown; the curtains and bedspread were of plain yellow linen—Delia hated what she called squiggles. With the exception of her mother's and sisters' photographs, the pictures were sporting in character, and foxes' masks and brushes, expensively mounted, further adorned the walls. On the bed lay a pair of serviceable striped silk pajamas and a woolen dressing gown. Delia stripped and, after a good wash at the fitted basin, put them on and sat down before her dressing-table to brush her hair. She wasn't vain and she professed a deep contempt for fashion, but she liked to look well-groomed.

She brushed her hair for ten minutes by her wristwatch; then she cleaned her strong, white teeth, tidied the room and went downstairs. With a word to John she opened the front door and went out, shutting it behind her. It had a Yale lock and one of the three duplicate keys was pinned in the pocket of her dressing gown.

It was a lovely night, thought Delia, as she walked across the sweep of the drive to the wicket gate. The thick summer darkness smelled of hay and there was something about the smell of hay . . . well, haytime wasn't like harvest—garnered fruit of earth and all that; it was a magic, moonshiny time, she felt rather than thought, for she wasn't apt with words: and it made you feel restless, even a little angry, the sweet wild never-to-be-recaptured smell of hay. I want . . . I want . . . I don't know what I want, thought Delia, but she did know. Years back, such enchanted nights had inspired in the forthright jolly girl the same longing, but fainter, sweeter and without this sharp savor of regret. Though she had always been the first to laugh heartily at sickly sentiment, there had been occasions when she had indulged her pretty dreams, but now her dreams weren't pretty, and, as she closed the wicket gate behind her and walked across the lawn, resentment stirred within her, and suddenly she hated life, that year after year sent rose and nightingale, set the scene for the drama in which she had no part. Forty-three? Behind your back, soft-footed, time fled by; soon there would be no more chances . . . oh, hurry, hurry, push, snatch, grab! As she took off her dressing gown, laid it across the foot of the bed and climbed in between the blankets, her thoughts trickled, then burst through the sluice gates of control. Surely she had shown him . . . surely he knew now . . . surely he would come. How else could she bear this scent of hay, the solemn silhouette of the fir trees, the blaze of stars in the dark velvet of the sky? She shut her eyes, but the smell was still in her nostrils and a little wind sighed among the branches of the firs. Why didn't he come? Had he misunderstood her, or was she so utterly undesirable? If that was it, he'd be sorry . . . she'd make him sorry . . . oh, listen, listen. . . .

What was it? She sat up, throwing off her blankets, clasping her knees, and the whistle came again, the double note, rising and falling, which is commonly used to attract the attention of an associate. Whi-whew! She swung her legs out of the bed, struggled into her dressing gown and, treading as lightly as possible, set off across the lawn. She opened the wicket gate without a sound, and, keeping near to the hedge, tiptoed across the gravel. There was light in the north still; the line of the stable roof cut the sky and she could see her way clearly, but she must be careful; *he* might have whistled, but there were other lovers. . . .

As she came to the end of the hedge, she heard a third whistle. She could always tell where sounds came from—even when hounds spoke deep down in the beechwoods, she was not deceived by echoes. She knew now that the whistle didn't come from the stable yard but from behind the stable. Well, that was a better place; the shrubs that bordered the back drive made it dark and secret. She crossed the yard, glancing back at the house; there was no light there and no sound but the soft familiar rustle of Flavia moving in the loose box. Ah, such a night for love, thought Delia, and she crept round the corner of the stable. . . .

SATURDAY

"YOUR COFFEE, DARLING."

"Oh, darling, thank you."

"Is it really just as you like it?"

"Yes, it's lovely, Sheila dear."

Since the demise of Humphrey Cathcart, breakfast at Marley Grange had been a bright and cheerful meal. To be grouchy at breakfast, Grace would argue, to grumble about the weather, the crops or the government, to withdraw behind a newspaper was antisocial and worse: it was rank ingratitude, she would continue, dropping her voice, to One Above. You had survived the perils of the night; you had your health and strength; and here was a new day with all its opportunities. . . .

Humphrey had never responded to these arguments: he had said for God's sake shut up, and for Christ's sake stop nagging; and that was such a funny way to go on, because deep down in his heart he must have known that Grace was right. However, he was gone now and, though Nancy had his fairness and Delia his voice and his love of horses, in character the girls were pure Ponsonby-Copes, and the Ponsonby-Copes had always been bright at breakfast.

At Marley Grange there was no nonsense about tomato juice or grapefruit; silver dishes containing eggs and bacon, some kind of fish and perhaps grilled kidneys were to be found keeping hot on the highly polished copper lazy man. There was a choice of tea or coffee, bread, scones or toast, and Delia was generally sampling a new kind of cereal. Every one attended to the needs of others before her own, and this caused some confusion and much chatter . . . "Darling, this was for you. . ." "No, you have it, darling. . . ." Delia was firm; Sheila in a muddle; like a ray of sunshine, Nancy flitted here and there.

When at last everybody had what she wanted, there was a lull before people started seizing one anothers' empty plates and carrying them to the side table, and it was then that Mrs. Cathcart, beaming on her daughters, would enquire, "Well, what are the plans for today?" This morning, however, a hitch occurred in her routine. Sheila had helped Nancy and her mother to coffee, Nancy had helped Sheila to eggs and bacon and her mother to kidneys, Nancy had poured out Sheila's tea and Sheila had placed a lightly boiled egg before Nancy, and now all three of them were sitting down at the table, but, as Delia had not yet entered the dining room, it was impossible to discuss plans. Mrs. Cathcart said a little peevishly, "Where's darling D.?"

"I don't know," said Sheila. "I didn't hear her in the bathroom so I called out of the landing window as I came downstairs. I thought she might have overslept. But she was up all right. Perhaps she got up early."

"Perhaps she's gone for a walk," said Nancy. "It's a lovely morning."

"If she had gone for a walk she would have taken John," said Mrs. Cathcart. "She was saying only yesterday that he needs more exercise. I suppose there's nothing wrong with the horses?"

"I can see Skylark," said Sheila, who sat opposite the window. She screwed up her shortsighted eyes and said, "He looks all right. And when I looked out on my way downstairs I could see that Ames was grooming Flavia. Perhaps D.'s gone mushrooming."

Mrs. Cathcart laughed. "You vague darling! There won't be any mushrooms for a fortnight or three weeks. And if she had gone out somewhere she would have been back by now. She's a Ponsonby-Cope for punctuality."

"Perhaps her watch stopped," suggested Sheila.

"It wouldn't be that. Delia's watch is always right," said Nancy.

"Let me take your plate away, Mother," said Sheila. "Then I'll run out and ask Ames if he has seen her. Or would you like another kidney?"

"No, thank you, darling. But I don't want you to interrupt your breakfast."

"I'll go," said Nancy.

"No, I'll go," said Sheila. She put her mother's plate on the side table and left the room.

The stable yard was flooded with sunshine. White fantail pigeons were cooing on the brown roof; a ginger cat stepped delicately across the cobbles. Ames was standing by the tap staring in front of him while Flavia's teak bucket filled and brimmed over. He was a dark, youngish man, who had been eighteen months in the Cathcarts' service.

"Oh, Ames," stammered Sheila, who was shy with servants, "have you seen Miss Delia this morning?"

The groom started out of his dream and turned the tap off. "No, Miss," he said, "I haven't."

"She hasn't come in to breakfast," said Sheila. "She's been sleeping out, you know." Sheila colored and went on hurriedly, "We wondered if she had gone for a walk or something."

"I haven't seen her, Miss," said Ames, lifting the bucket.

Sheila said, "Thank you," and turned away. She didn't like talking to Ames: she didn't like men; they lifted heavy buckets . . . their muscles swelled . . . they sweated. . . . She went back to the house. Jessie was in the lobby polishing the brass door handles.

"Oh, Jessie, have you seen Miss Delia?"

"Not this morning, Miss."

"She hasn't come in to breakfast."

"Well, I 'aven't seen her since last night," said Jessie sulkily.

Sheila went on to the dining room. Nancy and her mother were eating toast and marmalade. A shred of orange peel clung to the gray hairs on Mrs. Cathcart's upper lip. Sheila said, "Oh, Mother, a little bit of marmalade."

"Where?" asked Mrs. Cathcart.

"Just *there,*" said Sheila. "No, a little higher up. That's got it, darling. Neither Ames nor Jessie has seen anything of Delia."

"Oh, dear," said Mrs. Cathcart. "I hope nothing's happened."

"What *could* have happened?" said Nancy. "As D. would say herself, keep calm."

"She might have gone riding," said Mrs. Cathcart. "I know it's silly, but I'm always so nervous. Now I've finished," she said, pushing away her plate, "and I don't know what anyone's plans are."

"Perhaps I can help," said Sheila. "Delia was going to school Flavia before it got too hot, and then she was going to lunch at the Hall. In the afternoon you and one of us were going to tea at the rectory."

"One less to lunch and two less to tea. Which of you is coming with me?"

"I don't know. They said one of us. Perhaps Nancy. . . ."

"No, you go, darling."

"No, you."

"Perhaps Delia would like to go," said Nancy.

"It's very awkward," said Mrs. Cathcart. "We can't arrange *any-thing*. And I really am getting a little worried."

"Oh, darling, don't worry," said Sheila. "I daresay the maids know. I'll ring for Taylor."

Taylor was the parlormaid. The maids at Marley Grange were usually called by their Christian names, but Taylor's Christian name was Patricia and, as Delia had told her quite frankly, Patricia didn't *sound* like a maid. The girl had answered, "Well, then, Miss, suppose you call me by my surname. They does that in some places where they wants to look it and can't." Delia had asked her what she meant and Taylor had explained, "Oh well, Miss, people which wants to look big. . . ." Delia had asserted that she didn't in the least want to look big; it was just that Patricia was unsuitable, and Taylor had replied that she quite understood and that she wasn't like some girls: if anything wasn't right she liked it to be mentioned. So now here was Taylor, tall, pink-cheeked and blue-eyed, in a lilac cotton dress and a plain morning apron, and when Mrs. Cathcart asked her if she had seen any sign of Miss Delia, she said, "No, I haven't seen a sign of her, Madam, but she can't of gone far in only her pajamas and dressing gown."

"Oh, but didn't she come indoors?" said Mrs. Cathcart.

"I don't think so, Madam," said Taylor, looking at her nails. "Jessie popped into the kitchen just now and said that Miss Sheila was asking for her, and Elspeth said she didn't think Miss Delia could have used the bathroom this morning. She was up and down to the cupboard, she said, and she didn't see anything of Miss Delia. Then Jessie said that when she went to do the lobby the front door was shut. When Miss Delia comes in she always leaves it open, and the cat he gets in and forgets himself in Jessie's nice clean lobby."

Mrs. Cathcart said, "Tch, tch," about the cat, and "Well, I really don't know what to think," about Delia.

Nancy got up from the table.

"I shouldn't worry, darling. After all, what *could* have happened to D.? She's so very capable. If it had been silly little me, now. . . ."

"Or vague me," put in Sheila.

"Then you might have worried," said Nancy.

"Oh, I know Delia's capable," said Mrs. Cathcart, "but being capable wouldn't prevent her from being taken ill, would it, dear?"

She got up. "I'm sure that's it. She may have fainted and be lying anywhere."

"But, darling, she's never ill," said Nancy.

"What I think," said Sheila, "is that she came in and dressed and went out for a walk or down to the farm with a message—she was talking about getting some hay in for the horses, yesterday. She may have come in before the maids were up—you know what an early bird she is."

"I expect that's it," said Nancy. "On the night when she came in because it started to rain we never heard her."

"Excuse me, Madam," said Taylor, "but you could soon see if Miss Delia come in and dressed because of her clothes. I mean, they'd be gone, wouldn't they?"

"That's a good idea," said Sheila. "I'll run up and look."

"I'll go," said Nancy.

"I'll come too," said Mrs. Cathcart. "We've finished breakfast, Taylor, if you want to clear."

As the three women hurried upstairs, Sheila whispered to Nancy, "I do hope D. doesn't come in suddenly and catch us. She'll be furious if she knows that Mother is fussing like this." Nancy said, "I know. Let's hurry up," and she opened the door of the bedroom and called back, "No, she hasn't dressed," for Delia's jodhpurs were neatly folded on a chair and her shirt and tie were hanging over the back.

"Oh," said Mrs. Cathcart, "then she must be ill. She wouldn't have gone far in her dressing gown."

"She might have been wearing something else," said Sheila. "A cotton frock or her tweed skirt." She walked to the wardrobe and vaguely peered in.

"I thought," said Mrs. Cathcart, "that she was going to school Flavia."

"She might have changed her mind. It was very hot even before breakfast. Her gray tweed's here and her blue linen frock. Where's the striped one?"

"She wore that last week," said Nancy.

"Perhaps it's in the wash."

"If she had dressed, her pajamas and dressing gown would be here," said Mrs. Cathcart.

"Aren't they?" said Nancy.

"No," said Mrs. Cathcart, and her voice trembled. "Darlings, I *am* worried. The strongest people get appendicitis. I think we had better look round the garden."

"But, darling, if Delia had felt ill she would have come straight towards the house," said Sheila.

"Well, I don't know what to make of it," said Mrs. Cathcart, sitting down on the bed. "If Delia were here, she'd know what to do. She'd advise me. . . ."

"Oh, darling, don't look so worried," said Nancy tenderly. "I know what we'll do. You go down and order the meals as usual, and I'll take my little car and drive up the lane and down the road and round about. I bet you anything I shall meet Delia."

Nancy's little car had been a birthday present from her mother and sisters. She had always been nervous of driving the twenty horsepower Foxley, and, after five years of Delia's capable coaching, had still crashed the gears, dreaded reversing and insisted on handing over the wheel in the suburbs of Melchester. Delia had spoken sharply one day, and Nancy had wept, so Mrs. Cathcart had decided that the Foxley was too heavy for her baby's little wrists, and a secondhand eight horsepower car had been procured. It had been shabby then, and Nancy's habit of backing into stationary vehicles had not improved the condition of the fabric body nor the shape of the rear wings. The interior, however, was kept very neat by Nancy; she had sewn pretty loose covers for the seats; she had flowers in the vase on the dashboard; she loved her little car, and grew quite angry and obstinate if anyone suggested that she should change it for a newer model.

The little car was sacred to Nancy. No one else ever used it, so Sheila didn't suggest that she should go in it: she said, "Don't you go, darling. You might get lost too. I'll take the Foxley." But Nancy said, "Darling, I won't get lost. I shall come back quite soon to see if Delia has come in, which I'm sure she will do. And, don't you see, supposing she meets me in the little car she won't think anything of it—I can tell her a little white lie and say that I'm looking for flowers for a design to embroider. If she sees you in the big car, she'll know we've been fussing."

"Yes, that's true. But take care of yourself, darling."

"It's very kind of you, Nancy," said Mrs. Cathcart. "I know you think I'm a silly, nervous old woman. But you don't know what you three girls mean to me."

Nancy kissed her and went out. Sheila said, "She's sure to meet Delia, Mother. Won't you go down and do the ordering now?"

Mrs. Cathcart got up and walked uncertainly towards the door. "If you'll go and look round the garden, Sheila, dear."

"I will," said Sheila, "but I'm sure Delia won't be there. I mean, Ames and Appleyard have been working about the place since eight o'clock. But I *will* look." Clumsily but kindly she helped her mother downstairs.

Mrs. Cathcart went to the kitchen. She ordered the meals, writing the menu on a slate, but her thoughts were elsewhere, and it wasn't until she was rising from the table that she became conscious of the frigid atmosphere familiar to every housewife. "Is there anything else, Cook?" she asked nervously.

Mrs. Hemmings was small and, unlike most members of her profession, thin. She wore gold-rimmed spectacles, and her dark hair was parted in the middle and drawn back into a knot, which bristled with innumerable strong black pins. She gave an impression of timid decorum, which never failed to please her employers, but it was an erroneous impression; among her intimates, Mrs. Hemmings revealed herself as loud-voiced, bawdy and gay.

"Well, Madam," said Mrs. Hemmings, "I know it's nothing to do with me. This is your 'ouse, and of course you does as you please, but Jessie's the best girl for work as ever I 'ad under me, and now it seems as 'ow Miss Delia 'as give 'er 'er notice—last night it was—Miss Delia was ready for 'er when she come in. Of course it's nothing to do with me and you must please yourself, but you've never said a word about being dissatisfied with Jessie and when she told me, you could 'ave knocked me down with a feather, that you could. Jessie was doing the range this morning when I came down—half-past six that was, I'm not like some I could mention, I'm always up to time. Jessie says, 'Good-morning, Mrs. 'Emmings,' she says, and, 'Well,' she says, 'someone else'll be doing this 'ere range before long.' 'Whatever do you mean, girl?' I says, and Jessie says, 'Miss Delia gave me my notice last night when I come in.' 'Never!' I says, and Jessie, she says, 'Yes, Mrs. 'Emmings, that's as true as my name's Jessie Bix.' 'Well,' I says, 'and you the best girl for work as ever I 'ad under me. Whatever 'ave you been doing?' I says. 'I 'aven't done nothing,' she says. 'I was in the grounds when the clock went ten and then all as I did was to say good night to my friend.' 'Well, Jessie,' I says, 'Miss Delia wouldn't give you notice for that. Surely,' I says, 'she knows what young girls is when they're walking out.' But Jessie, she says no, and of course you must please yourself, m'm, but we shall never get such a clean girl as Jessie. Look at that Mabel we 'ad, and the Gladys before Mabel and the Gladys before that!"

Mrs. Hemmings paused, possibly for lack of breath, and Mrs.

Cathcart said, "Oh, but Cook, Jessie didn't tell you everything. That Albert Funge was with her, and he was abominably rude to Miss Delia."

"Well, Madam, Jessie did tell me that 'er friend spoke up for 'er, but that's natural, isn't it? And if 'e forgot 'imself a bit, well, we know what the men are. I'm sure my late 'usband . . ."

Mrs. Cathcart interrupted her. "Albert's not at all a nice young man."

"Oh, I don't know," said Mrs. Hemmings. "He's a lad, I grant you, but that sort often makes the best 'usbands."

"Well, that's neither here nor there," said Mrs. Cathcart. "The point is that Jessie was late, and not for the first time. I spoke to her myself the time before. I'm sure I mentioned it to you."

"You did say something about it," admitted Mrs. Hemmings, "but speaking's one thing and giving a girl 'er notice is another. I've always been one to stop, but I must say I don't like all these changes."

"Oh, well, Cook," said Mrs. Cathcart, alarmed, "I don't want you to get unsettled. Perhaps if Jessie promised . . . I'll speak to Miss Delia. You see, I haven't had a chance to talk this over with her. I suppose you haven't seen her this morning?"

"No, I 'aven't," said Mrs. Hemmings in a voice that added thank goodness.

"I'll speak to her when she comes in," said Mrs. Cathcart. "Well, that's all then." She stood for a moment fidgeting with the slate, and then trailed out of the kitchen.

Jessie's face peered round the scullery door. "Old bitch gone . . . ?"

"Now then, Jess," said Mrs. Hemmings, "you speak respectful. Yes, she's gone, and she says she'll talk it over with Skinny. I did what I could for you, girl, but then I'm not like some . . . now, you put the kettle on and let's 'ave a drop of wet. There's that chocolate cake . . . they won't remember that from Sunday. . . ."

"Coffee and a cream bun in a Melchester cafe is what I'm going to have this morning, thank you," said Jessie, with her head in the air. "Got to call in at the Registry Office."

"She didn't say you'd mentioned it, Jess."

"And supposing I 'aven't? I've accepted my notice and they can't stop me looking around. Well, I must go upstairs and tidy or I shall miss Albert and my lift in the Rolls Royce. . . ."

The little car drew up and the engine stopped. "Oh dear, I never can remember to go into neutral," said Nancy, and then she called out, "Is Delia back?"

"No," said Sheila, who had hurried out of the front door, and her eager face fell. "Oh, Nancy, I did hope you would find her. Mother is worrying so."

"I went all round the lane," said Nancy, "and back through the village. I asked lots of people if they had seen her. I'm afraid they'll think it awfully queer."

"We can't help that," said Sheila. "I must say, I thought at first Mother was making an unnecessary fuss, but look at the time now! I mean, it's getting on for eleven. D. can't have been wandering about all this time in her dressing gown."

"What *can* she be doing?"

"Something must have happened," said Sheila. "Mother wants to ring up the police, but I've persuaded her not to, so far."

"It would make such a lot of talk," said Nancy. "Do try to keep her quiet, Sheila dear. I'll go off again. I'll go towards Melchester and then back by the common this time." She started up the car, reversed into a tub containing a bay tree, stopped the engine, started it in gear and shot off down the drive.

Sheila watched her go, and then turned back into the hall. "Was that Nancy?" asked a plaintive voice from the top of the stairs.

"Yes, darling."

"No news?"

"No. But she's gone off to try again."

"I shall ring up the police," said Mrs. Cathcart, coming down.

"Oh, but darling, we decided that we'd keep calm till eleven. . . ."

"I can't keep calm any longer," said Mrs. Cathcart. "I know you mean well, darling, but you don't realize what a mother's feelings are."

"I'm sorry, darling," said Sheila instantly. "I'll ring up for you."

Mrs. Cathcart seldom spoke on the telephone. She suffered from a varying degree of deafness due to blockage of the eustachian tubes. She didn't imagine that she was deafer than she was, but she expected superhuman powers of hearing from non-sufferers, and when her daughters telephoned for her she would sit or stand beside them, making suggestions and asking what was being said. It was a maddening habit, but neither Sheila, Delia or Nancy ever snapped at her. "Just a minute, Mother," they'd say, or, "Ssh, darling."

Now Sheila asked for the police station and, as the operator repeated the number, Mrs. Cathcart said, "Is that the policeman?" "Not yet, darling," said Sheila. "You had better tell him that we fear an accident," said Mrs. Cathcart, "or perhaps it would be better if he came up at once and we could explain." "Ssh, darling," said Sheila, and into the mouthpiece, "Are you there?" "Is it him?" asked Mrs. Cathcart. "Is that the police station?" said Sheila. A loud voice, that Mrs. Cathcart could hear, said that Constable Haydon was speaking. "I should tell him to come up," said Mrs. Cathcart at the same time as Sheila was saying, "I'm speaking for Mrs. Cathcart at the Grange. We can't find my sister, Miss Delia Cathcart, and we wondered if any accident had been reported . . . ?"

"Tell him to come up," said Mrs. Cathcart.

"One minute, darling," said Sheila. Constable Haydon was speaking: "Accident to a cart, did you say? In the event of neither party wishing to make a charge and names and addresses having been exchanged, there's no occasion to report it."

"What did he say?" asked Mrs. Cathcart. "No," said Sheila down the telephone, "that isn't it. We want to know if there's *been* an accident. Miss Delia Cathcart is missing."

"Miss Delia Cathcart?" said the constable. "Oh, I see. Missing, is she? Well, we 'aven't 'ad no accidents reported, not since Friday the 24th ult. Her ladyship, that was, outside the Dog and Duck."

"What does he say?" asked Mrs. Cathcart.

"No accident has been reported," said Sheila, and to the constable, "We're getting a bit worried. What ought we to do?"

"Well, Miss," said the constable, "I don't rightly know. 'Ow long 'as the young lady been out?"

Sheila said, "We haven't seen her this morning."

"Tell him to come," insisted Mrs. Cathcart, so, interrupting the constable, who was saying that it was a nice morning and perhaps the young lady had taken it into her head to go for a nice walk, Sheila said, "Mrs. Cathcart would be obliged if you would come up to the Grange at once."

"Oh, I see, Miss. But I can't do that. I'm just setting off to an inquest at East Bearswood. Principal witness of an 'orrible accident under the influence."

Mrs. Cathcart said, "What's that?"

"Oh, said Sheila, "but couldn't you come up later? When'll you be back?"

"Couldn't say, Miss. Sometimes they're over sharp, and sometimes they drags on. I could get up in the evening for certain, Miss, but can't promise you before."

"He can't promise to come before the evening," said Sheila to Mrs. Cathcart.

"Why not?"

"He's going to an inquest."

"Oh, how very tiresome. . . ."

Constable Haydon was saying that most likely the young lady would be back before he was, so Sheila said, "Thank you. You'll be up as soon as possible, then," and she rang off. Mrs. Cathcart said, "Oh, you've rung off. Why didn't you tell him to call in on his way to the inquest, dear?"

"It's at East Bearswood," said Sheila. "That's in the opposite direction, you know. Anyhow, darling, there hasn't been an accident."

"How do we know?" asked Mrs. Cathcart. "It might have been out of his district."

"Well, darling," said Sheila, "shall I telephone to Melchester?"

"It would be very kind of you, darling. I know you think I'm a tiresome old woman."

"No," said Sheila, "not at all. I mean, it's after eleven." She took up the receiver and asked for Melchester police station.

A voice told her yes, an accident had been reported: a young lady had been found with her head in a gas oven—Edna Biggs, of 9 Abbatoirs Road. Recovering from a shock that had turned her face white, then crimson, Sheila, shushing her mother, explained that Miss Delia Cathcart was missing from Marley Grange, and the voice recommended that she should speak to Superintendent Dawes. The Superintendent was brief and businesslike. He asked for particulars, and gave an opinion that the young lady had not been long gone. Perhaps, however, he heard Mrs. Cathcart telling Sheila to tell him that she knew the Chief Constable, for when Sheila suggested that he should come over, he readily agreed. "He's coming, darling," said Sheila, replacing the receiver, "and police cars don't have to bother about the speed limit, so he'll be here in ten minutes or a quarter of an hour."

It was, however, a full half hour before the Superintendent arrived. Mrs. Cathcart spent the time in walking about the room discovering cobwebs and dust and alternately wondering if she had been silly to send for the police and whether it would be for the best if Elspeth as well as Jessie and probably Cook should go. Sheila stood by the window giving vague answers, and presently she saw the small, dark blue police car swing round the corner of the drive.

"Here he is."

Mrs. Cathcart wrote "Dust" on the top of the piano and put back a wisp of gray hair.

"He's taken half an hour. Go to the door, Sheila. It will only make talk if Taylor lets him in."

Sheila obeyed, and came back with the Superintendent behind her. Mrs. Cathcart gave him one look, saw uniform, height, breadth, steel-gray eyes and a firm chin, and immediately began.

"Oh, Officer, we're so worried. My second daughter, Miss Delia, has been sleeping out at night and last night she slept out and this morning she was nowhere to be found. We didn't get anxious till after breakfast; we kept on expecting her to walk in, but it's ten minutes to twelve now and there's no sign of her and where can she have got to in only her pajamas and dressing gown . . . ?"

"One moment, Madam," said the Superintendent, taking out a notebook and pencil.

"What did you say was the young lady's name?"

"Miss Delia Cathcart. My second girl."

"Age?"

"Forty-three."

"Oh, I see," said the Superintendent. "And she's been sleeping out. Where?"

"On the lawn by the drive. I'll show you."

"In a moment," said the Superintendent. "What time did the young lady retire?"

"She came into my room and said good night to me some time between half-past ten and eleven. She was later than usual because one of the maids didn't come in. My daughter waited for her and spoke to her and to her young man, who was abominably rude. My daughter told me about it and then she went to her room to get ready for bed."

"That would be about eleven, then. Has the bed been slept in?"

"I haven't looked," said Mrs. Cathcart. "Sheila, have you?"

"Yes," said Sheila. "It has been slept in. I mean it's all untucked. And the catch of the front door was down this morning. My sister always slams it behind her and takes a key with her."

"I see. Then it's pretty certain that the young lady went to bed, but there's no evidence of how long she stayed there. Now, Mrs. Cathcart, did there seem to be anything on her mind last night, or was she just as usual?"

"I'm sure there was nothing on her mind," replied Mrs. Cathcart. "She was just her usual cheerful self, wasn't she, Sheila? And if there had been anything wrong, she wouldn't have hidden it. We are a very happy family, Officer. Each of my girls has her own niche, of course, but any little worry is confided to Mother."

"I see," said the Superintendent. "That's unusual nowadays, isn't it? Of course, the young lady might have wanted to spare you, Madam."

"Then," said Mrs. Cathcart, "she would have confided in her sisters. They are very devoted. Sheila, you don't know of anything?"

"Nothing at all, darling. Besides, Delia isn't the sort to worry."

"No," said Mrs. Cathcart. "She has a very strong, direct character. I call her the man of the family."

"Then it couldn't be a nervous breakdown or anything of that description?"

"Certainly not," said Mrs. Cathcart.

Dawes was silent for a moment. Then he said, "I suppose there is no love affair—we have to ask these questions."

Sheila colored and turned back to the window. Mrs. Cathcart said, "Oh no. Nothing of that kind. My daughter's attitude to men is that of a comrade—no sentiment."

"I see," said Dawes. "Platonic. And had she any special . . . er . . . comrade?"

"She has a great many men friends," said Mrs. Cathcart. "You see, she hunts and she breaks in horses. Whom would you say, Sheila?"

"Well," said Sheila, "there are several. But they're only friends. I don't see what they could have to do with Delia being . . . away, this morning."

"Perhaps not, Miss," said the Superintendent. "But it's a question we always ask. Where nothing's outstanding, the only way we can get on is by exploring every avenue."

"Yes," said Sheila, "but I mean, it's too absurd. Why men friends and not women?"

Dawes said pacifically, "I daresay I'll come to the lady friends, but let's finish with the gentlemen first, please. Can you give me any names?"

"Well," said Mrs. Cathcart, "there's Captain Willoughby."

"We don't know him well," objected Sheila.

"He doesn't come to the house much," admitted Mrs. Cathcart, "but Delia must know him fairly well, dear; she calls him Michael. You see, Officer, the Willoughbys live at Lane End Farm and my daughter often rides home with Captain Willoughby after hunting."

"But," said Sheila, "he's married."

"That makes no difference," said Mrs. Cathcart. "I mean, I've explained to the officer that Delia's friendships are platonic. Then . . .

let me think . . . there's old Colonel Crabbe . . . again, horses and hunting are the mutual interest. Then my daughter, like the rest of us, is often at the rectory and the Hall. She organizes the village cricket and the Cubs, so she sees a lot of the rector and that nice Major Crouch, who runs the Scouts—I think he might be described as a great friend of hers. But of course, Officer, you quite understand: these friendships are founded on mutual interests."

"Quite," said the Superintendent, who was jotting down names. "Anyone else?"

"I can't think of anybody."

"And what about enemies?"

"Oh," cried Sheila hoarsely and her hands lifted in an ungainly gesture. "You don't think that anyone's done any harm to her?"

"I don't, Miss," said the Superintendent. "In fact, I shouldn't be in the least surprised if that door opened any minute and the young lady walked in as cool as a cucumber. But I've been sent for, and it's up to me to make the usual enquiries."

"Of course," said Sheila. "I quite understand. But I'm sure my sister hasn't any enemies. I mean, she does so much. Everyone respects and admires her."

"Yes," said the Superintendent, "but that's just the point, Miss. The more a person does, the more they're likely to come up against people. When I say enemies, I don't mean people who have gone about threatening the young lady. I mean someone she's had a little difference with, or a servant she's dismissed—something in that style."

"Oh," cried Sheila, her eyes staring behind her glasses. "Jessie and Albert!"

"What's that?" asked the Superintendent.

At some length Mrs. Cathcart told him of Jessie's disobedience and how Delia had mentioned that Funge had been abominably rude to her. Dawes made a note, observed that there was probably nothing in it, and asked if there had been any other unpleasantness of the same kind recently. Mrs. Cathcart remembered hearing Delia speak sharply to the groom, and then Sheila said, "What about Forbes?"

"Oh, yes, there was that," said Mrs. Cathcart. "What was it exactly?"

"We used to have Mr. Ross for our vet," explained Sheila. "And then he took an assistant called Forbes. He came about John—our spaniel—and Nancy—that's my other sister—saw him. Nancy thought he was quite good, and then he came about the horses, and Delia thought he was good till the last time. Something was wrong with a gray horse she had, and whatever it was—I don't understand horses—Forbes did the wrong thing for it. Delia said afterwards that he had been drinking. Anyhow, the next day he came again, and Delia had found out what was really wrong with Sultan and she told Forbes that she would tell Mr. Ross how careless he'd been, and they had rather a row. Delia said that Forbes was tipsy then, though it was only eleven o'clock in the morning."

"And did she report him?"

"I don't know. She said she was going to."

"Well, there's nothing much in that," said the Superintendent again. "Still, it's as well to know." He closed his notebook with a snap. "Now I'll see the lawn where the young lady slept out, if I may, please."

Sheila went towards the door, but Mrs. Cathcart hesitated.

"What will the maids think?"

"I'm afraid we can't bother about them," said the Superintendent, following Sheila.

They went out into the lobby. Sheila opened the front door and, as she did so, the little car, missing on one cylinder, came chugging up the drive. Nancy braked in gear as usual, said, "Oh, dear," and then as she looked out of the window and caught sight of the policeman, "Oh!"

"It's all right, darling," said Sheila. "Nothing's happened, only it got so late we thought we had better notify the police. I suppose you haven't found out anything?"

"No," said Nancy getting out of the car. "I've been all round the roads and nearly into Melchester. I've asked lots of people. You'd think—wouldn't you?—that dressed as she was, someone must have noticed her?" Nancy raised her forget-me-not eyes, brimming with tears, to the Superintendent.

Like most large dark men, Dawes was touched by small fair women. He said, "Don't worry, Miss. I haven't yet looked into the question of what she was wearing. We are just going to see the lawn where she slept out. I conclude," he added, "that this is another Miss Cathcart?"

"My youngest daughter," said Mrs. Cathcart. "Our home bird."

They passed through the wicket gate. Delia's camp bed stood on the lawn unmade and presumably just as she had left it. "That's good," said Dawes. "I was afraid that someone would've been tidying. You can see, Madam, that the young lady just threw the blankets back and got out—no sign of a struggle."

"Thank God," said Nancy. "I didn't say anything for fear of making you anxious, but when I went out early this morning I met such a terrible looking man. I'm sure he was a burglar."

"What time was this?" asked the Superintendent.

"I suppose I started about ten, didn't I, Sheila? I went up Lovers' Lane and back by the road because D. often goes that way just for a walk, you know. This man was walking along the road. He did look awful."

"I'll make enquiries about him," said Dawes, "but I shouldn't think there was anything in it. No burglaries have been reported in the district this side of Christmas, and it's a fact that very few burglars resort to violence. The man may have been just a tramp, Miss Cathcart. Some of them look rough customers, especially to a lady's eye, but they're generally quite harmless."

"Then what's your theory?" asked Sheila.

"My theory is that the young lady got up, put on her hat and coat—and underthings, of course—and went off somewhere."

"But where? We always discuss our plans days ahead," said Mrs. Cathcart. "Besides, none of us heard her."

"Would you have heard her?" asked Dawes, turning round and surveying the solid facade of Marley Grange. "That looks a well-built house; I noticed that the doors were good thick oak ones; and perhaps she didn't want you to hear her."

"We didn't hear her that night when she came in because it was wet," Sheila reminded her mother.

"There you are, you see, Madam. Now I should like to look at the young lady's bedroom."

As they filed indoors, heads in caps disappeared from the landing and the attic windows. Upstairs, Elspeth was clinking cans in the housemaid's cupboard.

"The upstairs work ought to be finished by now, Elspeth," said Mrs. Cathcart.

"Yes, m'm," said Elspeth. "But it's Saturday—my day for the cupboard."

"You can leave it till later," said Mrs. Cathcart, and with maddening deliberation Elspeth wrung out a floorcloth, picked up a bucket of soapy water and disappeared in the direction of the back stairs.

Mrs. Cathcart took the Superintendent into Delia's bedroom and Sheila and Nancy remained in the corridor. Presently Mrs. Cathcart called to them, "The officer wants you to tell him if anything's missing."

Blushing deeply, Sheila walked into a bedroom with a man in it who wasn't a doctor.

"There isn't," she said shortly. "I looked through the wardrobe."

"And what", said Dawes, "about underclothes?"

"I can hardly tell that," said Sheila. "I mean, there would be things in the wash and so on."

"Shoes?

"Her bedroom slippers aren't there, but then they wouldn't be. Oh!" said Sheila, looking under the dressing table, "Where are her blue suede shoes?"

"Ah, now we're getting hot," said Dawes.

"Perhaps," suggested Mrs. Cathcart, "they are in the ottoman with her other London clothes."

At the foot of the bed stood a wicker ottoman, gilded and covered with brown and yellow cretonne. "I gave each of my girls one last Christmas. I meant them for their hats, but Delia keeps all her best things in hers." She opened the ottoman and Sheila, peering over her shoulder, said, "Yes, her blue flowered frock is gone and her hat. And the shoes aren't there, are they?"

"How very extraordinary," said Mrs. Cathcart.

"Reassuring," said the Superintendent, "I should say. And what about the dressing gown and . . . er . . . night attire? If you haven't seen anything of that, I think it's obvious that the young lady took some luggage along with her."

Mrs. Cathcart said on a rising note, "But Delia wouldn't go away without telling me. . . ."

"Of course not, darling," said Nancy.

"But supposing she had," said Dawes, "what suitcase or handbag would she be likely to take?"

"Either her rawhide suitcase or her dressing-case," said Nancy. "The rawhide, I should think. The dressing-case was fitted with silver things and rather heavy."

"Where did she keep them?"

Sheila went towards the fireplace and opened a built-in cupboard. "Here, with her riding boots and things. Oh, the dressing-case is here . . . and her hat box . . . but the suitcase isn't. . . ."

"Well then," said the Superintendent, "I think that's clear. The young lady came in from the garden, dressed, packed her suitcase and went off wherever she was going. Probably some of the girls heard her."

"If you mean the maids, they didn't," said Mrs. Cathcart. "We asked them."

"What time do they get up?"

"Cook was down by half-past six."

"And the rest," said the Superintendent flippantly. "Anyhow, the young lady came in early and evidently she didn't want you to know that she was going away. I shouldn't upset yourself at all, Madam. You'll probably get a letter first post tomorrow." His manner had changed. He smiled as he spoke and his gray eyes twinkled.

"But where can she have gone? And why? It's so unlike Delia."

"Young ladies will be young ladies," observed Dawes.

"I don't know what you mean by that," said Sheila.

"Oh, well, Miss, I mean you never know. . . . But, if you ladies don't feel like waiting till you hear from Miss Cathcart, I should try round among her friends. All of us get tired of family life sometimes, and perhaps she took it into her head to plan a jaunt—Paree or somewhere—and thought that you mightn't quite approve."

"Not like Delia," quavered Mrs. Cathcart.

"You never can tell, Madam. The best of us kick over the traces at some time. Well, I must be getting back to the station. Perhaps you would give me a ring there and let me know that it's all OK."

"But aren't you going to do *anything?*" asked Sheila.

"About tracing the young lady? I'm sure it's unnecessary, Miss— not a police job at all. Of course, I've got all particulars, and if you don't hear from her in a day or two, you must let me know."

"What I don't see," said Sheila, "is how she could have got any- where. She didn't take the car."

Dawes said, "There's buses. But it's much more probable that whoever she went with picked her up at the end of the drive here in his car."

"*His* car . . . ?"

"Or *her* car," said Dawes hastily. "Or *their* car, as the case may be. You try round among the young lady's friends, Miss, especially if there are any of whom Mrs. Cathcart didn't quite approve. I must be off now. Good morning, Madam. Good morning, ladies. You'll let us know."

He walked resolutely out of the bedroom and downstairs. The three women heard his car start, roar down the drive and hoot at the entrance, before they spoke again.

"What do you think he thinks?" asked Nancy.

"I hate him," said Sheila furiously. "He thinks that our darling Delia has gone off with some man."

"What can you expect?" said Mrs. Cathcart. "Men have such horrid minds. You don't know, darlings. . . . No girl would get married if she knew what men are."

"Not all men, surely," said Nancy. "He's common; I mean he must have started as an ordinary policeman—an elementary schoolboy. . . ."

"They're all the same," declared Mrs. Cathcart. "But never mind what he thought. We'll find our darling Delia ourselves."

Sheila said, "But how?"

"Well," said Mrs. Cathcart, "the only sensible thing that horrible man said was about ringing up our friends. Of course, I don't see why Delia should have gone to any of them without telling us, or why she should have started off at such a queer hour, but perhaps she thought of something important that she had forgotten to tell someone, and then she got delayed. But then, why did she take her night things . . . ? Oh, dear."

"Darling," said Sheila getting up from the ottoman, where she had been sitting in one of her ungainly attitudes. "Let's not bother so much about the 'why' as the 'where.' It's getting on for lunch time. I suggest that we have lunch early and then start ringing up people. Everybody will be at home having lunch then."

Mrs. Cathcart agreed and Nancy ran downstairs to ask that lunch should be served as soon as possible. As it happened to be Mrs. Hemmings's afternoon out, she was only too happy to oblige, and the gong rang before Mrs. Cathcart had finished tidying her dishevelled hair. At lunch Sheila and Nancy made conversation for the benefit of Taylor's obviously pricked ears, but when she had put the biscuits and cheese on the table and withdrawn, they discussed whom they should ring up and what they should say. Sheila volunteered to do the telephoning, and Nancy said she would look up the numbers, and then both of them besought their mother to go and lie down. Mrs. Cathcart, however, declared that she couldn't rest till she knew where Delia was, and obstinately followed her daughters to the telephone.

Sheila rang up the rectory. She didn't, she said, very much like prevaricating to the rector, by whom she had been confirmed, but Mrs. Cathcart assured her that what she was saying was only a white lie. So Sheila said that Delia had gone out and not come back when she was expected and her mother was getting worried in case she had had a crash in the car. "You know what the roads are nowadays," said Sheila, laughing nervously. No one at the rectory had seen anything of Delia. Then Lady Angela between a furious "Damn those dogs," and "Shut up you blasted bitch, can't you?" declared that she hadn't seen Delia either while she had been out riding this morning or at the Hall. The Misses Hepburn hadn't seen Delia and avidly hoped that nothing was wrong. Colonel Crabbe hadn't seen Delia since the fete on Saturday, and Major Crouch hadn't seen her since Wednesday evening, when she had been the only sane person besides himself at the committee meeting. Sheila said wearily, "That's the lot except for the Willoughbys."

"I should call those her nearest friends," said Nancy. "I mean, among the local people. Of course, there are plenty of others further afield—in London, for instance. But people would think it so queer, wouldn't they?"

"Besides," said Sheila, "if she had gone far, she would have had to hire a car or take a bus. If we think she's done that, it would be best to get the police to trace her. The Willoughbys are seven one, aren't they, darling?"

Mrs. Willoughby answered the telephone. She had a clear deep voice, which Mrs. Cathcart and Nancy could hear easily.

"Yes?" she said. "Yes?" But when Sheila said that it was Sheila Cathcart speaking, she said, "Oh, yes, what is it?" in a dull, flat tone.

Sheila asked if by any chance anyone at Lane End Farm had seen anything of Delia, and the voice, suddenly deep again, boomed out, "What? Has she gone too?"

"Well, she went out and she hasn't come back, Mrs. Willoughby. Mother's getting a little worried in case she's crashed—so many accidents nowadays. But has . . . . anyone else gone?"

"Oh, no," said Mrs. Willoughby. "At least . . . .oh, no, there couldn't be any connection. It's nothing at all. Oh, no. No, we haven't seen anything of Delia. In fact, I haven't seen her since the day I had tea with you. Only yesterday, was it? Sometimes I lose all sense of time. She can't have been taken ill, can she? She looked the picture of health, then."

"No, she's been quite all right," said Sheila. "By the way, how are *you*? I ought to have asked, only you know what it is . . . we're so worried."

"When I fainted? Was that only yesterday, too? Do you think it can have been premonition? It's so unlike me to faint. How kind you all were! I do hope you will soon have news of Delia. What time did she go?"

"Don't tell her, dear," hissed Mrs. Cathcart. "She's such a gossip," so Sheila said down the telephone, "I don't quite know—fairly early."

"It wasn't very early, was it?" asked Mrs. Willoughby. "I mean not before breakfast . . . ? And she didn't leave a note, did she?"

"Why?" asked Sheila, while her mother hissed again, "Don't tell her." "I mean, Mrs. Willoughby, do you know anything? I mean, we should be so glad of the slightest clue . . . so grateful. . . ."

"She did go before breakfast, then," said the deep voice, growing shriller. "And so did Michael. He's gone, too."

"Good heavens!"

"Yes, he's gone. It's all those horses . . . just because I'm too highly strung, too nervous to ride! Horses, horses, horses!" shrilled Gerda Willoughby, "all day long! And that sister of yours is the same. . . ."

Sheila's face was scarlet.

"It's not true," she said, and then, "Mother, Nancy, she says that Captain Willoughby has gone away."

"I heard her," said Mrs. Cathcart. "And I was thunderstruck. Did she dare to insinuate that my Delia . . . oh, let me speak to her."

Sheila handed over the receiver. Mrs. Cathcart said, "Mrs. Cathcart speaking. Mrs. Willoughby, do I understand that because your husband has left you, you are impudent enough to suggest that my daughter is with him? Are you there? Hullo, hullo, is that Mrs. Willoughby? Oh, she has rung off, has she? Thank you." Mrs. Cathcart replaced the receiver. "She's rung off. What will the Exchange think?"

"I've never liked her," said Sheila.

"Next time I meet her I shall look through her," said Mrs. Cathcart. "Or else I shall give her a look that she will understand. Darlings, forget what she said. She sounded quite hysterical. Who else is there?"

"There's Major Carruthers," suggested Sheila. "He likes Delia, you know. At the fete he spent over five pounds at her stall. And, being the Chief Constable, he might give us some advice."

"I rather hesitate," said Mrs. Cathcart, "to worry him. I mean, he's real county, besides being a military man."

"I expect he'd think us very silly," said Nancy. "The police did, didn't they?"

"Yes," said Mrs. Cathcart, "but the police aren't gentlemen. And the Major's got a kind face. What do you think, Sheila?"

"I think it would be a good thing, darling."

"Very well. Get on to him, darling, will you? And then I'll speak myself—that would be more courteous. I'll tell him a little more than I told the others. He has a kind face, and he's always taken notice of me at bazaars. Oh, is that Major Carruthers?" said Mrs. Cathcart into the telephone. "Oh, Major Carruthers, we are a little worried about my second girl, Delia—the riding one. She hasn't come back and we're ringing up our friends to find out if she's with any of them."

Besides his face, the Chief Constable's voice was kind, and, after they had talked for a few minutes at cross purposes, Mrs. Cathcart told him the whole truth. "We called in the police," she said. "I hope you don't think it was silly of us. But all that your man could suggest was that Delia had gone for a jaunt with some friends in a car. Of course she wouldn't do that. We are a very united family, Major, and she'd realize how worried we'd be. Then that Mrs. Willoughby—her husband left her this morning and I don't wonder at it, but she had the audacity to suggest that Delia is with him."

The Chief Constable's kind voice said, "Tch, tch. I should think that most unlikely, Mrs. Cathcart. I'd put the odds at a thousand to one against it, any day. I mean, your daughter doesn't strike me as that sort of . . . er . . . girl. Rides straight at her fences, what? Besides, I should imagine that Willoughby's tastes would run to quite a different type. Bit of fluff, what? Not your daughter's type at all."

"Then what do you suggest we should do, Major Carruthers? You see, Delia is our adviser. I call her the man of the family, and we're quite at a loss without her."

"I know it's worrying, but you can only wait, Mrs. Cathcart. Wait and hope, what? Most likely you'll hear from her."

"That's what your man said. He said we'd hear by the first post tomorrow. He seemed to think that she'd gone to Paris—I can't think why."

"Figure of speech, I expect," said the Chief Constable. "Gay Paree, what? Of course he doesn't know your daughter, probably pictures her as a modern type of girl. But I shall be in Melchester this afternoon, Mrs. Cathcart, and I'll call in at the police station and study the particulars and have a chat with Dawes. I must say that in the general run of things I should take the same attitude, but Miss Delia always struck me as a particularly levelheaded reliable stamp of . . . er . . . girl."

Mrs. Cathcart talked a little longer about Delia's character and then about a mother's feelings, which the Chief Constable said that he understood perfectly, only he'd got a fellow to lunch and must buck up if he was going to get into Melchester. Mrs. Cathcart said good-bye and rang off and sank back in her chair. "I expect you got the gist of that, darlings," she said wearily. "Now, as dear Major Carruthers says, all we can do is to wait and hope; and," she added, thinking suddenly of that queer God whom she kept on a string and fed and exercised at the proper times, "pray. . . ."

MONDAY

IN THE KITCHEN at number six Jasmine Grove the radio had been switched on since nine-thirty; the next-door terrier, aware that his master had returned from work, was rattling his chain and yelping in anticipation of a walk round the gasworks; in some further back-yard a bantam had laid an egg and was loudly cackling; at the end of the road trams, grinding out to Streatham, tinged impatiently; every now and then the house shook as an electric train thundered beneath it.

"And naw fer a bit of England, 'ome, and beauty," said Jim Huggins.

"Don't you start getting fresh, Jim; not in this 'eat," replied Mrs. Huggins.

With a grunt of contentment, Jim Huggins sat down in a Windsor chair and bent forward to unlace his boots. "Yer right. It tis 'ot. All very well fer them 'oliday-makers, but it gets me in the feet."

"If you perspired freely, same as I do, you wouldn't feel it so much," replied Mrs. Huggins, wrestling with a tin of sardines. "Naw the key's gone and bust, but that's nothing new, is it?" She turned over the tin into a saucer patterned with rosebuds. "There, mister, yer tea's ready."

Besides the tea there was a white loaf, half a pound of margarine, a slice of Canadian cheddar, some beetroot swimming in vinegar, a pot of strong tea, a jug of thin milk, a basin of lump sugar, a cold boiled onion, and seven fancy cakes on the table. Mr. Huggins liked his tea tasty. Sweet things played up his teeth. The fancy cakes were for Mrs. Huggins, who never ceased to laud the day when, at the age of twenty-one, she had had all her teeth extracted.

Mr. Huggins got up, placed his boots on a shelf in the scullery, pulled a pair of felt slippers over his gray worsted socks, unbuttoned his uniform coat and took off his tie and his collar. Then he sat down at the table and sucked the last shreds of the ham sandwich he had had for lunch from his teeth, while he surveyed the fare provided.

"Wot'll you 'ave?" said Mrs. Huggins.

Mr. Huggins answered by cutting a slice off the loaf, spreading it with margarine, mashing up a liberal helping of broken sardines and heaping them on it. He helped himself to a chunk of cucumber and half the onion and tipped into his plate the saucer which held the beetroot. Then he spoke: "Lettuses is cheap. Yer might of got us a nice lettus."

"Ar," said his wife, "it ain't cheap to buy maggots. But that's men all over, looks at the outsides an' no further. Same as when they're courting."

After a long day's work, Mr. Huggins had no taste for polemics. He changed the subject.

"'Oliday crowds beginning."

"Ho, really. I thought nobody left London till after the Eton and 'Arrer."

"It ain't that sort yet. It's city workers; staggering, they call it. Like carrying their bags for themselves." Mr. Huggins assumed a mincing accent. "No, thenk you, portah."

"Tries to look it and can't," said Mrs. Huggins.

"Yer right." Mr. Huggins smelt the cheese and then helped himself to a slice. "Wot's that noise on the wireless?"

"They calls it music," said Mrs. Huggins scathingly. "Yer got in too late fer the talk. Nice voice 'e 'ad. The news'll be coming on in a minute."

"News? There ain't no football this month," Mr. Huggins complained gloomily.

As he spoke, the last item in a program of Elizabethan music drew to its sprightly close and a pleasant self-satisfied voice announced that before the news here was a police message. *"Missing from her home at Marley Grange, near Melchester, since Saturday morning, the second of July, Delia Margaret Cathcart, aged forty-three, five feet four inches in height, gray eyes, fresh complexion, slim build, believed to be wearing a printed silk dress, navy blue hat, and shoes and to be carrying a rawhide suitcase, stamped with her initials. Will anybody who has any knowledge of her whereabouts communicate with the Melchester Police Station, telephone number, Melchester 23, or any police station.* "

"After 'er bit of fun the same as the rest of us," Mrs. Huggins commented.

"Old enough to know better," said Mr. Huggins. "Raw'ide? A lot of them about nowerdays," he added professionally.

Mrs. Huggins helped herself to the last of the fancy cakes. "No use keeping 'em till they're stale," she remarked in parenthesis. Then, "I shouldn't fancy raw'ide myself."

"I don't suppose as it's really raw. Any'ow, no rawrer than other leather. Light-colored so as to look different. Come to think of it, one passed through me 'ands only yesterday. Left on the rack. I took it along to Lost Luggage."

"Yer'd never believe 'ow careless some people are!"

Mr. Huggins was thoughtfully packing his pipe. "Funny about that there suitcase. It must 'ave been the one o'clock slow. Now where does thet come from? Woking; but where before thet? Melchester's down beyond Woking. Passenger might of got in there. Though why anyone should want to travel from Melchester slow, only Gawd Almighty knows."

"And 'E won't split," said Mrs. Huggins. "Perhaps they got out at Woking."

"They might of."

"Delia Margaret and something beginning with C. I suppose yer didn't 'appen to notice the initials."

"In a manner of speaking I did." Mr. Huggins lapsed into painful thought, while his wife cleared the table. "For Gawd's sake, Win, 'ave yer finished? I can't seem to get my mind working with you lumbering around."

"Lumbering?" cried Mrs. Huggins. "It ain't my fault I ain't slim built."

"I ain't blaming yer. Even at yer best, yer weren't no glamor girl."

"And you ain't no Gary Cooper." Mrs. Huggins lifted the tin tray and carried it into the scullery.

Jim Huggins cast his mind back. He could see the suitcase, the solid leather and strong shiny plated fastenings; he could feel the weight of it in his hand. He would have bet confidently on the weight, cautiously on the measurements, but, though he was almost sure he had noticed initials, he couldn't visualize them. Presently his wife came back into the kitchen. "Well 'ave yer cast yer mind back?"

He shook his head. "Not thet it really matters."

"Naw, isn't thet just like yer? Don't want a reward." Winnie Huggins wasn't really avaricious, but there were one or two things— a matching tea service, a sideboard like her sister, Elsie's, a pair of nice vases for the mantelpiece—that she could do with.

"There ain't been no mention—so fer; and I shall deal with the matter termorrer," replied Mr. Huggins, becoming official. "If them initials is right thet case'll be opened if I 'ave to ring up the perlice."

Mrs. Huggins' natural caution reasserted itself. "Naw, Jim, don't yer go getting yerself mixed up with anything. And if they do open thet raw'ide case, don't yer go getting too near—it may be a torso. . . ."

Since British working men and minor officials do not err on the side of precipitation, it was noon on the following day before a raw-hide suitcase, stamped with the initials D.M.C., was opened with all due authority at Waterloo Station. It was found to contain: one pair blue silk pajamas, one blue kimono, one pair satin bedroom slippers; brown lace evening dress and brown velvet coatee; one set of peach-colored underclothes; two pairs of silk stockings; one pair green evening sandals; one maroon evening bag; one pair silver brushes and tortoiseshell comb; one sponge bag, containing sponge, face flannel, toothbrush and powder.

WEDNESDAY

DETECTIVE-INSPECTOR GUY NORTHEAST, of the C.I.D., sat in a third-class carriage and gazed sullenly through the window, which the elderly lady opposite had asked him to close. He had passed through the emulous little heaths of Surrey into the pleasant farmlands of Hampshire and corn was ripening and bullocks fattening, but neither the beauties of nature nor the prospect of a satisfactory harvest could brighten his mood of black despondency. He was crying for the moon. Like many another he was asking to be given back an hour, which had long since passed into that exasperating unimaginable nowhere where the flame of the candle goes—the hour between nine and ten of that blasted Monday morning, when with heaven knows what ideas in his silly young head he had dashed out of Aunt Millie's house in Raynes Park, where he had been stopping over the weekend, and had traveled, hurrying from tram to bus and from bus to underground, to enlist in the Metropolitan Police Force.

Guy Northeast was the fifth child and third son of a Wiltshire farmer. For three generations the Northeasts had farmed Thorn End. Roger, the eldest son, would follow his father; Jim was developing a successful sideline breeding and breaking hunters; Pam managed the poultry; Dinah ran the dairy; and when Guy, at the age of sixteen, drank two glasses of port after Christmas dinner and suddenly found he had courage to ask his father if he could go to Canada and be a Mounted Policeman, he was firmly told there was plenty for him to do on the farm. Guy at sixteen had been big, slow and speechless—a perfectly helpless person in spite of his broad shoulders, iron biceps and huge red hands. He had given up his dream of

50

tracking desperate criminals over snow-covered canyons, and had settled down to do all the jobs that were beneath Roger's dignity, spoiled Dinah's hands, got on Pam's nerves, or bored Jim. After four years of it, he threw a turnip at Roger and went to stay with his Aunt Millie while the storm died down.

Millie Northeast had married beneath her. She had married the head footman at the Towers; but Thomas had prospered, and he and his wife now owned a private hotel inhabited by old ladies and young male clerks. Millie had therefore no hesitation in recommending her nephew to strike out on his own, and she did not consider that to be a constable on point duty was an unfitting occupation for a yeoman's son. She pressed Guy to stay on with her and correspond at a safe distance with his family, and after several heated letters had passed between Thorn End and the Walmer Private Hotel, he received a grudging admission that it was no use crying over spilt milk; what was done was done; and, if he liked to lower himself, he was welcome. In three months Guy was thoroughly homesick, tired to death of hearing people say, "Northeast? Ha-ha! I'd sooner have Southwest," and fed up with his work, which he found agonizingly monotonous after the varied and hypothetical work of the farm. He possessed, however, his fair share of the admirable vice of false pride, and he stuck out the first dull years, and presently discovered, to his intense surprise, that his common sense, good manners and ability to act on his own initiative had, after all, been noted by his apparently unimpressionable superiors. He was transferred to the C.I.D. and luck was with him at first, but, since he had been promoted to be Detective-Inspector, it had deserted him; he had bungled the Oughborough case, and believed it wasn't by chance that since then only dull routine enquiries seemed to come his way.

Now he was traveling through Hampshire to investigate the disappearance of a spinster of uncertain age, who was obviously suffering from sex repression. "Nothing much in this, Northeast," Superintendent Hannay had said. "Of course, the bag turning up at Waterloo may indicate that she is in London; otherwise there's nothing that Melchester couldn't handle. However, the Chief Constable down there seems to be a friend of the family and he's been pulling strings here—got a wife who's got a brother who's got a wife who's got a husband. You'd better take the bag down and get it identified and look round a bit. I expect you'll get a pretty frigid reception from the blokes at Melchester."

So Guy, looking out of the window that he'd been weak-minded enough to shut, was wishing he had remained a farmer. Roger had been irritating, but not half as irritating as a succession of sergeants, detective-inspectors, superintendents and assistant commissioners; when Guy's father had died, he had left him a thousand pounds and that would have been enough to start farming in a small way on his own. A farmer's life was disheartening, but at least he was his own master; as a policeman, however high you rose, you always had someone above you, someone to look down his nose at you, thinking of Lady Oughborough's emeralds and Flash King's acquittal, and saying, "There's nothing much in this, Northeast," and meaning even you can't bungle such a simple little case as this. . . .

The train slowed down. The old lady who had wanted the window shut asked if she was right for Melchester, and Guy said she was, and lifted down her luggage, and the luggage belonging to a respectable young person in gold spectacles, and the rawhide suitcase with the initials D.M.C. and his own substantial brown leather one. The train drew up, and he carried his bags to the exit and out into the station yard. Outside the station were four or five taxis, a bus from Marley-in-the-Marsh and several decrepit cars attached to trailers containing pigs or poultry; girls in tweeds with spaniels at their heels were anxiously enquiring for hampers from the agricultural show at Lesser Pocklington. Guy, realizing that if he wasted no time he might catch an afternoon train back to London, blowed the expense and took a taxi to the police station, where he asked for the Superintendent. A moment later he was shaking hands with a rather frigid Dawes, who eyed the card he presented with suspicion.

"Well, Northeast, I don't see why they should have troubled you with this little affair. Girls will be girls—even in the provinces."

The omission of his rank, obviously with intent, and the somewhat unnecessary stress on the word "provinces" showed him that he must be tactful. He said, "Quite so, sir, but our experience is that girls from the country are rather inclined to get into trouble in our wicked city."

"Why should you assume that Miss Cathcart is in London?"

"Because her suitcase was found there, sir," said Guy, making an effort to show the respect that the Superintendent clearly expected from a mere inspector.

Dawes beat a tattoo with his pencil on the table while his slow brain worked. "What evidence have you that the bag you've found is Miss Cathcart's?"

"Well . . . it's made of rawhide and it's got the right initials."

Then, realizing that he might have to work for a time with this self-opinionated provincial, he added in a conciliatory tone, "But that's not what you or I would call evidence, Super."

"Your first job is to get it identified, Northeast."

"Yes, that's why I was sent down and because somebody seems to have been pulling strings."

"That Mrs. Cathcart; she seems to think no one has anything better to do than to be at her beck and call. If you don't find the daughter soon, she'll write to the Prime Minister or the Archbishop of Canterbury."

"Mightn't a mother like that make a daughter want to leave home?" asked Guy thoughtfully. "You know, Super, there's a lot in this case that doesn't open and shut."

"So Scotland Yard's trying to make a puzzle of it, are they?" sneered the Superintendent. "You can take it from me, Northeast, the young lady—though she's no chicken, really—has found a gentleman friend to be kind to her for a nice long weekend. Suppressed sex, that's what it is."

"Then why did she leave her luggage on the rack of the carriage?"

"Just came over flustered, never having been naughty before."

"Ye-es; that's possible, I suppose. Did anyone happen to notice her at the station?"

Superintendent Dawes was rather taken aback. "That's an angle that needs investigating, of course. I'll have that looked into while you're trotting out to Marley Green with the suitcase." He got up to show that the conference was ended, but Guy had not come all the way from London to be so cavalierly ushered out of an office.

"There's not a great deal in this suitcase; I mean not exactly a trousseau."

"Packed in a hurry—never having been naughty before."

Guy still sat firm. His chief in London wanted a report, and trivial though this case might be it was his duty to make a thorough investigation while he was about it. "Have you any objection to my making a few routine enquiries of the family and servants while I'm at the house?"

"You can waste as much time as you like; it won't affect our county rates." Then softening slightly, Dawes added with an air of generosity: "I'll lend you my notebook; that'll give you something to read on the bus."

"Thank you. And when should I get back?"

"There's a bus about five that'll give you time to pay a few calls—you'll see I've jotted down some names in my notes. I'd advise you to see a certain Mrs. Willoughby and ask her a few questions. I understand from the Chief Constable that her husband left her on Saturday, and, if I wanted to *cherchez*, I'd *cherchez* for the gallant Captain. Now, if you want to catch the Little Hitherford bus, you'd better be getting along to the Town Hall."

This time Guy took the hint. "Right you are, Super. Seeing as I'll be seeing you again, do you mind if I leave my own suitcase here?"

"You'd better, Northeast. It'll be a damn sight safer than on the rack of a bus." The Superintendent's grim face relaxed as he chuckled at his own joke.

So Guy took the Little Hitherford bus and bumped out to Marley Green smelling hay and reading the Superintendent's notes. After asking his way at the Dog and Duck, he walked down the dusty road and turned in at the white gate of Marley Grange.

The drive, with never a weed in it, led him past the stable yard, clean as a new pin; bearing right it widened into a sweep of golden gravel under the short north wall of the house. On his right ran a tall yew hedge, newly clipped; and on his left was a broad herbaceous border and the apple orchard beyond. Evidently, he thought, there's someone about the place who knows how to keep the servants up to their work, and he thought, what an unlikely setting for any kind of tragedy! He walked up to the front door and pressed the electric bell, noticing how bright the brasses were, how spotless the paint work. A fair-haired maid in a brown uniform promptly admitted him. He followed her through the cool hall into the drawing room.

Sheila Cathcart was sitting at the piano. Coming through the hall he had heard what sounded like classical music, and hoped this wasn't going to be the sort of case you read about in novels, where the detective knows that the victim couldn't have been in the music room at the time stated, because so great a musician would never have played Puccini. The sun, streaming in through the south windows, turned Sheila's lovely auburn hair to a flaming aureole; he imagined her beautiful, and was conscious of disappointment when the maid gave his name and she turned towards him and he saw an ugly woman.

"Oh," said Sheila, getting up, blinking, blushing, hugging her elbows. "You're the detective from London—Scotland Yard, aren't you?"

"Yes," said Guy. Sheila's shyness was infectious. He blurted out,

"Detective-Inspector Northeast. I've brought a suitcase—just to see if you can identify it."

"Yes. Oh, yes," said Sheila. "Mother's very anxious."

Guy said, "Superintendent Dawes doesn't think there is much to worry about. Excuse me, but are you one of the Miss Cathcarts?"

When he had first come into the room, Sheila had thought him one of the most attractive men with whom she had ever been brought into contact. While she had blinked and blushed and held her elbows, she had been wondering if he were married, if his wife understood him, if he realized that a pretty face isn't everything. The night would be dark and full of nightingales . . . no, not nightingales . . . that would mean waiting for a whole year. The night would be dark and still. "Oh, Sheila," he'd say, his voice trembling with passion. "Oh, Sheila, what do mere looks matter—it's your soul I love, your deep dark soul, so full of music and beauty. . . ." She was conscious of disappointment when he said, "Excuse me, are you one of the Miss Cathcarts?" and she realized that he wasn't quite a gentleman.

"Yes," she said. "Oh, yes. I'm the eldest Miss Cathcart. Sheila. The musical one."

"I see. Well now, Miss Cathcart, I wonder if you have formed any theory of your own?"

Sheila fidgeted with the music stand.

"We've talked it over such a lot . . . don't think what that Superintendent Dawes thinks. He thinks that Delia has gone away with friends or a friend—abroad probably. I know she wouldn't. You see, we're not a modern sort of family. We're very devoted to one another. Apart from that, my mother's heart's not strong. Delia would have realized that anxiety like this might kill her."

"Then you rule out that theory absolutely?"

"Absolutely."

"And what do you think of this—that she was suffering from loss of memory?"

Sheila gave a mirthless laugh.

"You don't know Delia! She's never had a day's illness. She doesn't know what nerves are. Now if it were me . . . I mean, I'm artistic and artistic people are always highly strung, aren't they? Delia is a most matter-of-fact practical person. She hardly ever opens a book. Only the evening before she disappeared we were talking about the artistic temperament and she said she didn't believe in it; she said it wasn't temperament, but temper."

"Oh! Was there an argument about that—any unpleasantness?"

"No. Oh no. Delia said that none of us were artists, so it didn't matter."

"That was rather tough on you, wasn't it?"

Sheila smiled sadly. "Well, you know the saying about a prophet being without honor. . . ?"

"Yes," said Guy, and wondered how many tiresome people had fed their vanity on that particular proverb. "I suppose you realize, Miss Cathcart, that you're only leaving one possibility—foul play of some kind?"

Sheila blinked.

"I know. It's terrible. We can't think of anyone who could have wanted to harm Delia. But she was sleeping out there and there are maniacs, aren't there? And there was the tramp my sister saw."

"Yes. He's down in the Superintendent's notebook. I'll make a point of enquiring if he's been traced. But tramps are a harmless race as a rule."

"He may have been drunk . . . !"

"Yes; that's a possibility, of course. But then he'd have rolled into a ditch and stayed there. I don't think there's anything in it, Miss Cathcart, really."

Sheila seemed unconvinced. "My sister said he was an awfully rough man and very dirty."

"That doesn't make him a murderer. I mean," he said hastily, seeing Sheila turn white, "if it's foul play you suspect, you must look among people who knew your sister. You mentioned one or two names to the Superintendent—a young chauffeur named Funge and a veterinary surgeon called Forbes, both of whom might have had some sort of grudge against her."

"Yes. Funge is a horrid young man, and he was very rude to her. Forbes we mentioned because he was quite tipsy once when he came here and she threatened to report him to the vet he works for."

"Neither of them seems to have very strong motives. Still, I'll see both of them. Now, Miss Cathcart, I wonder if you'd look at this suitcase."

He went out into the hall, tripping over John, who was asleep on one of the Persian rugs which were spread across the parquet. Back in the drawing room, he asked Sheila, "Did you hear anything from the dog on the night of your sister's disappearance?"

"Nothing at all. He sleeps in the lobby, but he's rather old and deaf and I don't suppose he'd hear anything that happened outside. Of course, if Delia did come in to dress, he would have recognized her footstep. Yes, Mr. Northeast, this is her suitcase."

"Will you open it?"

Sheila opened the case and went through the contents, murmuring, "Dressing-gown . . . slippers . . . evening dress, evening shoes . . ." but modestly remaining silent when she lifted out the underclothes.

"It's just what she would have packed for a couple of nights, isn't it?"

"Yes," said Sheila.

"But supposing she was . . . well, going away with a man friend, she'd have packed more, wouldn't she?"

Sheila was up in arms at once.

"Do you mean that you think the same as the Superintendent?"

"Oh, no," said Guy, trying to look innocent and, because he did think it and had the sky-blue eyes which overdo everything, not succeeding. "I'm just trying to prove once and for all that she didn't. I mean, somebody going away on an unofficial honeymoon would have packed . . . well, more frilly, seductive things, wouldn't she?"

"It would depend on taste," said Sheila. "Delia didn't care for frills and lace on . . . things, anyhow."

"I see. I suppose she didn't care for powder and scent and stuff like that, either?"

"No, she didn't. None of us do. We're not at all modern," said Sheila proudly.

The betraying blankness came into Guy's blue eyes again. He said, "Well, I'm afraid I must take these things back to Melchester with me, but you can claim them later, of course. Now, do you think I could see Mrs. Cathcart and your other sister?"

"Mother's in bed. She's absolutely worn out with anxiety. But if you really want to see her, I expect she could get up for a little. I'll ask her, and in the meantime you could see Nancy, but please, please don't say anything about foul play to her. You see she's the youngest, and she's always been our baby."

Sheila left the room. She walked badly, he noticed; you could almost say she shambled. He wondered if Delia were like her; if so, this Captain What's-his-name must have a queer taste in women. Of course, Sheila was absolutely the type for a Bride in the Bath—a repressed spinster, who had practically given up hope of any sex life—an easy prey for any man. He must find out if these women controlled their own money. . . .

The door opened softly and Nancy crept into the drawing room. Guy experienced the usual male reaction: faced with a small fair woman, he felt huge and protective. While Nancy looked fearfully up at him, he took matters into his own hands and said, "Good morning. I believe you are Miss Nancy Cathcart."

"Yes," said Nancy in a soft voice that shook a little. "Won't you sit down? You've come about Delia, haven't you? Would you like to smoke or anything?"

Infinitely preferring Nancy to Sheila, Guy sat down and said that unfortunately he wasn't supposed to smoke when on duty. The first question that he put to Nancy was: "Is Miss Delia Cathcart like you or like your sister?"

"Oh, she isn't like either of us," said Nancy. "She's dark, you know. She generally wears tailor-made things. I mean, you'd know that she was an out-of-door sort of person."

"And you're not?"

"No. Mother calls me the home bird," said Nancy.

"And do you like being the home bird?" said Guy chattily.

"Oh, yes. I'm rather nervous of things like driving cars, and of horses, and strange people. Of course I know it's silly."

Guy, whose philosophy was Mr. Browning's, except when his stomach was empty, thought it was very silly. But it was pathetic too, he thought. To be out of tune with life must, he thought, be awful. He said kindly, "Oh, well, some people do feel like that," and then "What do you think has happened to your sister?"

"I think she's gone away," said Nancy. "She took her suitcase, didn't she? That's it on the table, isn't it? Major Carruthers rang up to tell us it had been found in a railway carriage. I suppose she put it under the seat or on the rack and forgot it."

"Does she often forget things?"

"No, she doesn't. If it had been silly me, now. . . . But perhaps she was excited about something."

Guy said, "It's been suggested that she went away with a Captain Willoughby, who's also missing."

"I know," said Nancy. "It makes Sheila and Mother furious if anyone says so. But I'm different. I think that if people are in love . . . oh, I suppose I'm silly!"

"I don't think your sister was actually shocked by the suggestion. My impression was that she thought it would be so unlike Miss Delia."

"It would in a way. Delia was *friendly* with men. She thought that to be anything else was silly and sentimental."

"I see."

"Sheila's rather like that too," said Nancy, and Guy thought, oh yeah? "But I'm not. I daresay it's silly, but I look up to men."

Guy thought, oh lord, I shall have to get married. Married people talking and talking about their children aren't half as bad as celibates talking and talking about themselves. He said, "Oh, well, it takes all sorts to make a world," and then he said briskly, "I wonder if you'd come and look at the things in the suitcase."

Nancy said, "Delia's things? Oh, I couldn't! I know it's silly, but I couldn't."

"I know it's painful," Guy said kindly, "but really, I wish you would. I want to know if you think it's what she would have packed if she had been going away with . . . well, a man she loved."

Nancy said bravely, "Oh, that's different. If it will help, I must."

Holding her lower lip between her small white teeth, she went to the table. Guy, standing beside her, could see the gray in her fair hair, the light pucker of lines at the corners of her eyes, the pale coarsening hairs on her upper lip . . . yes, in strong sunlight the youngest Miss Cathcart looked fully her age. Guy was sorry for her; she was a gentle little thing, ought long ago to have found someone to look after her. "Well," he said, "is that all you'd have expected her to take with her?"

"For a night, or perhaps two nights—yes. But you'd think . . . oh, of course she must have walked, mustn't she? So she wouldn't have wanted to carry any more, would she? Perhaps she meant to buy all new things in London or wherever she was going."

"That's what I think. Do you know if she took much money?"

"She took her handbag, of course. At least, it's not in her bedroom. I know she cashed a check in Melchester on Saturday. And of course, I mean, men usually pay for most things, don't they?"

Guy laughed, and rather unfortunately at that moment the door opened and Sheila looked in. Her eyebrows rose. She said, "Mother's just coming down."

Guy heard a querulous voice saying that Elspeth had left a duster on the radiator and that nothing went right now that Delia was away. Then the door opened again and Mrs. Cathcart came slowly in. Guy thought she looked old and ill, but he couldn't, of course, tell how the anxiety of the last few days had aged her. Her wispy hair was neglected—merely tumbled together and insecurely fastened by innumerable black pins; the tortoiseshell slide, which she wore at the back of her head, was unhooked and so was the white net vest, which she wore inside the v-shaped neck of her gray dress. Her faded eyes were rimmed with red; a network of purplish broken veins stood out on the yellow parchment of her cheeks.

Guy was kind to old things. Long ago he had missed two seasons' hunting because his father had said that if he bought a new pony, old Snowball would have to be destroyed; he had never owned a fascinating puppy, but always old dogs that had grown too decrepit for successful Roger or dashing Jim. He looked down at Mrs. Cathcart and said, "I'm really awfully sorry that you should be bothered again."

Mrs. Cathcart looked at him and didn't approve. She had expected Scotland Yard to send quite a different looking person, someone small, sharp, alert-looking, a ferret of a man. Guy was not at all like a ferret; he looked kindly, calm and slow. With considerable loss of confidence, she said, "Of course I have to be bothered. I expect to be bothered. The local police have done nothing, but fortunately I know the Chief Constable and my cousin, Mrs. Gilbert Mountjoy-Harrington, knows the Home Secretary too." She paused to allow this threat to sink in, and then she said sharply, "Well, what are your deductions so far?"

"So far," said Guy, "I have only spoken to your daughters. I want to look over the house presently, and there are one or two people— young Funge, for instance—whom I shall interview this afternoon. Now, Mrs. Cathcart, I wonder if you would tell me exactly what your daughter said about the unpleasantness with Funge?"

With extraordinary incorrectness Mrs. Cathcart repeated her last conversation with Delia, after which she confirmed Sheila's opinion that Delia would never have run off—as she called it—with any man. Nor would she have left home in a temper; she was never in a temper; nor was it in the least likely that she would suffer from loss of memory. Guy asked how, if she suspected foul play, she could explain the fact that Delia had come indoors, dressed and packed a suitcase, and Mrs. Cathcart replied dramatically, "A false message! She must have been lured." But who by, and what for? Guy asked her and got, "That is what I expect Scotland Yard to explain."

So Guy shut his notebook and in the briskest tone that he could command said that he would like to look round the house and garden now. Nancy showed him up to Delia's bedroom, and the first thing he did wag to ask her to stay there and walk about, quietly but not on tiptoe, and open and shut the ottoman and the wardrobe and the chest of drawers and the cupboard by the fireplace, while he listened from her own room. With the doors closed, he heard very little noise, certainly not enough to wake a sound sleeper, nor did the door of Delia's room groan or the boards creak when, in obedience to his instructions, Nancy walked softly down the stairs. "Thank you very much, Miss Cathcart," he said. "I'll carry on now."

While Guy carried on, Mrs. Cathcart sat with her daughters in the drawing room. She said that Inspector Northeast didn't look at all intelligent and what could he possibly learn by going through Delia's clothes that Delia's mother couldn't have told him? Sheila said that it was a pity that Inspector Northeast was so common, and Nancy said that she supposed it was silly, but she didn't think that class mattered, only, as Mother had said, it needed brains to detect things, and Inspector Northeast only looked brave and kind. At that moment Guy came back. He was looking puzzled, and Mrs. Cathcart was more than ever disappointed with him.

He said, "Does Miss Cathcart keep all her clothes in her bedroom?"

"Yes," said Sheila, "except for her mack and Wellingtons. They're in the lobby with ours."

"There's no other cupboard where she'd be likely to hang anything?" he asked.

"No," said Sheila. "None."

"What about the bathroom?"

"We never leave any of our personal belongings in the bathroom," said Mrs. Cathcart. "It's so suburban."

"I see," said Guy, in rather a subdued voice, because he always left everything in the bathroom. "And when did the laundry go?"

Mrs. Cathcart said impatiently, "As usual on Friday afternoon about two."

Guy seemed set on homely details. He asked, "Do you have anything washed at home?"

"My housemaid washes stockings and handkerchiefs. The between-maid rubs through the dusters and tea-cloths every day. All the other things go to the laundry. The Melchester Sanitary Laundry. They are very inefficient, but we've tried every laundry in the district and they're all the same."

"Quite," said Guy, looking more puzzled than ever. "Well, I'll just look round the garden and then I won't trouble you any longer. By the way, the Superintendent tells me that Funge is employed as chauffeur by a Mr. Hislop at a house called Fairview. Is that far from here?"

Sheila directed him to a house on the Green, and he took his leave. Carrying the rawhide suitcase, he walked in at the wicket gate and stood staring thoughtfully at the lawn. Presently he strolled on to the stable yard. Ames, the groom, was in the forage room, mixing a feed, and Flavia's fine thoroughbred head peered greedily over the loose-box door.

Guy went up to Flavia and stroked her warm, satin neck. Ames looked out of the forage room and Guy said, "Nice type of mare."

Ames replied, "Ar." He came out into the yard carrying a bucket. Guy waited till the restless mare was quietly feeding. Then, as Ames seemed disposed to remain in the box watching her, he said, "I'm a police officer, making some enquiries about Miss Delia Cathcart and I should like a few words with you."

Ames picked up his bucket, ran his hand over the mare's quarters, opened the door and bolted it behind him in a leisurely insolent way. Then he turned and his hot dark eyes ran over Guy.

"I can't tell you nothing."

Guy said firmly, "You can answer a few plain questions." He didn't altogether like the look of Ames and he wondered why Delia Cathcart had engaged him. The man was very dark and, though a dark type was to be found here and there among the fair-haired, blue-eyed people of the county, his height, handsome features and reckless bearing disowned that persistent strain of early British blood. Half a gypsy, Guy thought, and perhaps a wizard with horses, but all the same he wondered that a lady engaging a groom hadn't preferred a more obviously respectable type of man. He asked, "How long have you worked for Mrs. Cathcart?"

"Miss Cathcart, I works for."

"Well, how long have you worked for Miss Cathcart?"

"Eighteen months."

"Was she satisfied with you?"

"Satisfied? Ar," said Ames with a look that the detective described to himself as sly.

"Are you married?"

"Wot the 'ell 'as that got to do with you?"

"Look here," said Guy quite pleasantly, "I'm a police officer and don't you forget it, my man."

The groom's eyes dropped. He said sullenly, "I bin married over three year."

"Where do you live?"

"In the cottage t'other side of the lane. Brick cottage with a slate roof wot wants seeing to, only they're that mean."

"What time do you get here in the mornings?"

"Eight o'clock."

"Were you here to time on the morning that Miss Cathcart was missing?"

The groom hesitated for a moment. Then he said, "Nearer a' past it was that morning. On account of 'aving overslep', it was."

"When you came, did you see anything of Miss Delia Cathcart?"

"Miss Delia? No, I didn't. The first of 'em as I sets eyes on was Miss Sheila. She comes out and asks if I seen Miss Delia, and I says, no."

"On the mornings when you arrived punctually—did you ever see Miss Delia then? Since she's been sleeping out on the lawn, I mean."

"No, that I didn't. I takes care to keep well on this side of the 'edge. I knows my place," said Ames with a sardonic grin.

"And did you ever hear anything of her? Anything like the latch of the gate falling, or her footsteps on the drive?"

"No, I didn't. I'd be getting on with my job, not listening for 'er fairy footsteps. One or two mornings I've caught a glimpse of 'er at 'er bedroom winder, trying to dress mutton up to look like lamb."

"But that particular morning you didn't see her?"

"No. It was only by chance that I ever seen 'er. I've no call to look towards the 'ouse. Old maids like them three ain't no treat to me."

Guy said, "You don't speak very respectfully of Miss Cathcart."

"Well, 'oo are they?" asked the groom. "Biscuits they was before they come 'ere. 'Owsoever, I 'adn't no complaint and nor, I reckon, 'ad she."

"All right," said Guy. "I think that's all for the present except a routine question: where were you during the evening—the Friday evening, that'll be."

There was a tiny pause. Then, "At the Dog and Duck, I reckon, till closing time. Then 'ome."

"I wonder what made you oversleep," said Guy.

"There was a chap standing drinks. Won a prize in a plowing match, 'e 'ad. Reckon 'twas the beer."

"I see," said Guy. "That's all then. Good day." Conscious of the nostalgic smell of stables, he walked across the yard, past the midden and along a grass-grown drive to a five-barred gate, from which he could see the groom's cottage, hung with clematis, on the opposite side of the lane. Behind the thorn hedge a haggard woman in a blue apron was taking washing from a line.

Guy crossed the lane and walked up the garden path. The sun

was beating down on the fertile half-acre; the air was heavy with the scent of clove carnations, reminiscent, soporific and warm. He thought of police stations that smelled of disinfectants and offices that smelled of ink and he sighed as he walked between a row of peas, heavy with lily-green pods, and runner beans, just showing their scarlet blossoms, twisting and twirling upwards towards the sun.

"Excuse me, are you Mrs. Ames?"

The haggard woman turned. She was as dark as her husband, but she looked years older. Her swarthy skin was engraved with lines of discontent and weariness; an attempt at a smile disclosed a mouthful of broken, rotting teeth.

"Yes," she said. "What is it?"

She had a gentle voice and the accent of another county—Dorset, perhaps, or Devon. Guy said, "I'm a police officer investigating the disappearance of Miss Cathcart. I've just been talking to your husband."

She turned away and took a garish overall off the line before she answered.

"What did 'e tell you?"

"He couldn't help me much," said Guy guardedly. "From my point of view it's a pity he overslept that morning. Why didn't you call him, Mrs. Ames? You were up, weren't you?"

"I was up at six sharp. Saturday's my day for the rectory washing. Wash, wash, wash. You can do too much for men," said Mrs. Ames bitterly.

"So you jolly well let him sleep?" said Guy, catching the mood of the exasperated wife.

"That's it. Served him right, it did. Them as stays up half the night can't expect to rise in the morning. Why should I wait on 'im? There's others as gets the fire kindled and a cup of tea brought up to them."

"Quite right," said Guy. "But all the same, he wasn't as late as all that, was he? I mean, coming in at night. The Dog and Duck closes at ten thirty."

"At the Dog and Duck, was he? Huh!" said Mrs. Ames through her pinched nostrils.

"Well, that's what he told me."

"I daresay he did. But the Dog and Duck doesn't stay open till three o'clock in the morning. I like a glass of beer myself, but it isn't beer that he stays out after."

Hell has no anger like a woman scorned, thought Guy, and he

thought that probably in a few hours this mood would pass and Mrs. Ames would remember that Tom, or Dick, or whatever his name was, was her lawful husband and had given her a bottle of scent on her birthday. Striking while the iron was hot, he said, "Who is the woman?"

"Anyone 'e can get 'old of. 'E ain't particular," said Mrs. Ames, viciously tugging down a pajama jacket.

"Village girls?"

"Ah, and not only them, I reckon. There's a funny lot round 'ere. Old maids, what would do anything to get 'old of a man, even to sleeping out in gardens."

"D'you mean Miss Cathcart?"

Mrs. Ames picked up her washing basket and bag of pegs. "I don't name no names," she said virtuously.

"It's wiser not," Guy agreed. "Well, Mrs. Ames, I see you want to get on, but there's one thing more. From your upstairs windows you can't see over the stable roof, I take it, but you can see the drive, can't you? You didn't notice any suspicious looking characters hanging about that morning, or anything funny?"

"Not that I knows of. First thing I heard of anything being wrong was when Stanley come 'ome for dinner. 'E says,'They're in a rare stew this morning. Old Delia's missing.'"

"Well, I must get on, too," said Guy. "Thank you for answering my tiresome questions."

"You needn't worry," said Mrs. Ames, walking along the garden path with him. "She'll turn up all right. I expect she got tired of being single. Some folks don't know when they're lucky," she added wearily.

Guy went out of the little green gate and, turning to his left, along Lovers' Lane until it joined the high road, which ascended to the Green, where thatched cottages, once occupied by laborers, had been enlarged out of all proportion and converted into desirable old world residences. He located Mr. Hislop's house, Fairview, and then crossed the Green to the Dog and Duck, where he lunched on bread and cheese, washed down by a pint of bitter. The landlord of the Dog and Duck was a depressed old man, who had been groom at the Hall, he said, in the days when Lord Danvers had kept twenty or thirty hunters. Oh yes, he agreed, Miss Delia Cathcart rode well, but he could remember Marley Grange before them Cathcarts came there. It was the dower house of the hall then, and the Dowager Countess had lived and died there, and the Cathcarts were good people, but of course they weren't the same class: they'd *made* their money. The shameless snobbery still obtaining in agricultural areas, took Guy a long way back; all honor, he said, to those who got on in the world, but Mr. Hogmore was right; with jumped-up people, you never knew where you were. Hogmore agreed. Now take these Cathcarts—no girls ever stayed any length of time with them, and look how Miss Delia had served old Black—her groom he was, and she'd sacked him for no better reason than because that good-for-nothing fellow, young Stanley Ames, had caught her eye. Hogmore wouldn't want to be in Ames's shoes, ha, ha. And now Miss Delia had gone off no one knew where nor wherefore and there'd been a police message on the wireless and goodness knew what would come to light. Hogmore wasn't one to gossip, but he knew where he'd start looking for Miss Delia.

Guy said that *he* wasn't one to gossip, but he'd heard remarks passed about a certain Captain Willoughby; what sort of a fellow was he? Captain Willoughby, Hogmore said, was as nice a gentleman as you could wish to work for, as openhanded as they are made. Tied up to the wrong woman he was; Hogmore's niece was cook at Lane End Farm and she could tell some tales. Mrs. Willoughby was as jealous as a cat, and carried on something awful if the Captain so much as looked at another girl. Bad all round it was, Hogmore considered, when married persons couldn't agree.

Guy agreed. Even a worm would turn, as the old saying went, and you couldn't blame the man if he *had* gone off with Miss Cathcart. Did Mr. Hogmore think there was any truth in that tale?

Hogmore wasn't naming no names, but that was about it. He'd always set his face against scandal and slander, but, between him and Guy and the bedpost, he blamed Miss Delia. No doubt she'd made the running, and the Captain, well, he was only a yewman being when all was said and done. Mr. Hogmore rambled off into a discourse on the frailties of yewman beings, and Guy, who was feeling sleepy and stupid after his pint of bitter, sat listening to him till the clock in the Norman tower of Marley church struck two. Then he paid his small bill and walked back across the Green to Fairview.

Mr. Hislop's house had once been a humble cottage with the decent name of Watkin's Pightle, but all that was changed now. A Tudor-style wing thatched with Norfolk reeds had been added; a garage to match had been built at the wrought iron gates; a gravel drive swept where once a mossy little path had wandered between marigolds to the door. Mr. Hislop was house proud and a great gardener; the rose beds, the gravel and the turf were weedless, and when Guy rang the bell the door was immediately opened by a spruce manservant in a white linen jacket, who sharply enquired, "Yes, sir?"

Guy shook off his postprandial lethargy. He asked for Mr. Hislop and was shown through a spotless hall into the garden. Mr. Hislop was gardening. He was tying dahlias to stakes. He had a hard, withered little face, and was wearing a Panama hat, gardening gloves and overalls. When he saw Guy, he stepped out of the dahlia bed and said testily that he never bought anything at the door.

Guy explained himself. Mr. Hislop was obstructive. He said that if a silly woman chose to give way to her nerves, he didn't see what it had to do with his chauffeur. If Funge was going to answer questions, he said, he should answer them in his own time and not in the time for which Mr. Hislop paid.

Guy referred to Mr. Hislop's duties as a citizen and after a sharp argument received permission to interrogate the chauffeur at the back door. He walked past impeccable dustbins and found Albert Funge sitting in the kitchen with his feet on the table, drinking tea.

When Funge heard that Guy was a police officer, he took his feet off the table and tried to please. He was a short young man with oily hair that smelled of violets and from his conversation it was evident that he thought himself a cut above the majority of the young men of Marley Green. He admitted that on the night preceding Miss Cathcart's disappearance he had had a few words with her, "but," he added, "I'm not like some of 'em round here; if I had noticed anything out of the way like, I should 'ave notified the police."

Guy said, "I understand that the unpleasantness arose through your lady friend not getting in to time. Miss Cathcart told her off, and then you chipped in, and Miss Cathcart threatened to report you to your employer. Mr. Hislop seems rather a particular sort of gentleman. What would have happened if Miss Cathcart had written to him?"

"Nothing much. Mr. 'Islop don't 'old with women. In any case, it wouldn't 'ave troubled me. There's always plenty of jobs for smart chaps what can speak nice and 'ave got the clothes."

Guy's dislike for Funge deepened. He said, "You don't seem to have spoken nice to Miss Cathcart."

"People gets what they asks for. She's got a bullying way with 'er. Gets your back up."

"I know what you mean," said Guy amiably. "Miss Cathcart doesn't seem to be very popular in the village, but of course it doesn't follow that anyone wished her harm. Now you seem to be an intelligent observant sort of a fellow. As you walked down the drive that night, did you notice what lights were on at the Grange?"

Funge considered. "One came on—that 'ud be Jessie's. I reckon there were two or three on before."

"You didn't stop about then—to see if your young lady was all right, I mean?"

"No, I didn't. I went 'ome."

"Straight home?"

"I say," said Funge, "what are you getting at? I didn't 'ave nothing to do with Miss Cathcart's disappearing act, if that's what you're suggestin'."

"I'm not suggesting anything," said Guy innocently. "But if you'd hung round a bit, you might have noticed some little thing. Where do you live?"

"Number two, Council Cottages. Down beyond the church there."

"And did you notice what the time was when you got in?"

"It was eleven to the tick. I know that's right, because Mother's got a lovely mi'ogany clock, and she sets it by the wireless of an evening and it always keeps good time."

"That's all then," said Guy. He wished Mr. Funge and the manservant, who, with his head bent over the sink, had been listening curiously, good day, and then he walked off along a path at the side of the house, which led him into the drive. Mr. Hislop was waiting for him.

"Well, Detective Inspector? Did you discover any important clues?" he asked sarcastically.

"I didn't expect to," said Guy, his slow Wiltshire voice as pleasant as ever. "But Funge was one of the last people to set eyes on Miss Cathcart, so he had to be questioned."

"Waste of the ratepayers' money," snapped Mr. Hislop. "In any case, you couldn't have believed what he told you. Man's a born liar."

"Really? Then I rather wonder that you go on employing him. I'm told that, just now, first-rate chauffeurs are two-a-penny."

"I shan't be employing him when his month's up. I gave him notice last Wednesday. Found him out in a lie. Can't bear liars. That's why I can't stand women."

"What did he lie about?" asked Guy, wondering if he would get an answer, but Mr. Hislop, with a grievance to air, had forgotten about the ratepayers' money.

"Last Saturday—wait a minute, was it Saturday? Yes, it was the day that neurotic woman chose to walk off—well, last Saturday he went into Melchester with the shopping list as usual, and he had the cheek to give his young woman a lift in my car without my permission. Friend of mine—good man, good gardener, but can't grow dahlias—well, he saw them and told me of it, and when I questioned Funge he denied it. Born liar."

"This was on the afternoon of the Saturday?"

"No, the morning. Come to think of it, what was the young woman doing out? Skivvies don't get out in the morning. There you are, you see. You can't trust women."

"Quite right, sir, you can't," said Guy cheerfully. "And in the end—did Funge admit it?"

"Yes, he did. Started to defend himself, but I wouldn't listen. 'If you'll tell one lie,' I said, 'you'll tell another.'"

"I don't blame you," said Guy. "Well, Mr. Hislop, I must get on. I don't suppose I shall need to trouble you again. This all seems quite satisfactory."

He went out through the iron gates and, under the cover and shade of a group of elm trees, stopped to make a few entries in his notebook. There was one more visit he wanted to pay before returning to Melchester, and some small boys, who were playing stump cricket, were able to direct him to Lane End Farm. It was about a mile away, they said, down Pitcher's Lane and, in answer to another question, yes, the next bus but one to Melchester did go from the crossroads at ten minutes to five.

Guy set off down Pitcher's Lane, which wound between tall hedges bordering pastures and hayfields. He wasn't a man who allowed his work to nag at him, and he found plenty of interest in a walk which a townsman might have found boring. He noticed that the hay had no bottom, admired a sow, coveted a mare and foal, was shocked by a rabbit warren and the state of the hedges. Presently he came to a five-barred gate, where a rutted track led up to a comfortable farm house standing among outbuildings. He turned up the track and made his way to the front door, which was standing open. From three different directions three Cairns, a Jack Russell and two spaniels flew at him.

Guy liked dogs and dogs liked him, and he had made firm friends with all six by the time that his knock was answered. Mrs. Willoughby came to the door herself, and when he told her that he was investigating Miss Cathcart's disappearance, she beckoned him into a small front room shabbily furnished as an office.

Mrs. Willoughby was tall and dark. She had large velvety brown
eyes, a discontented mouth and a sallow complexion. She wore an
orange smock over a black satin skirt, black satin shoes with rubbed
toes, and no stockings. She indicated a chair, took a low stool herself, and produced cigarettes from a crumpled yellow packet. She
said in a deep voice, "This is a ghastly thing, Mr. Northeast, or should
I call you Detective-Inspector? I don't think I can. I shouldn't feel I
was talking to an individual. I'm like that. I've no use for facades. I
must speak soul to soul. Of course, it's all these horses."

"Horses?"

"Yes! Horses, horses, horses!" cried Mrs. Willoughby with her
hands to her head. "That's what I told Mrs. Cathcart. Horses, horses,
horses! If it hadn't been for horses, my husband would still have
been with me, but it was horses, horses, horses, all day and all night."

"I see," said Guy gravely. "Captain Willoughby likes horses and
you don't. I suppose horseflesh was the bond—if there was one—
between him and Miss Cathcart?"

"Yes," said Mrs. Willoughby. "Actually, until Mrs. Cathcart rang
me up and asked if I'd seen her daughter, it hadn't occurred to me
that he had gone away with a woman. I thought it was just a kink—
I've heard of lots of men with kinks, who just left home for no real
reason at all. When I heard that Delia Cathcart had left the same
morning, I jumped to the conclusion that she was with him. I'm
frank to a fault, Mr. Northeast, and I'm afraid Mrs. Cathcart guessed
what I was thinking and, I must say, her reactions were sordid to a
degree. However, since then, I've been thinking the whole thing over,
and I'm almost certain that I'm the Only Woman, as far as Michael is
concerned. I'm not vain, but, you see, Mr. Northeast, I can give a
man so much—beauty, intelligence, passion—even if I can't talk about
horses."

Guy made an assenting noise, but kept severely to the point.
"You say Mrs. Cathcart rang you up about her daughter: are you on
very friendly terms with the family?"

"Oh, no. At least, the Cathcarts may think so, but to me friend-
ship means a real, deep feeling, not just going out to tea with one
another and talking of this and that. The Cathcarts are very nice
people, but, though the eldest sister plays a little, they're not *intelligent*. . . ."

"In fact, you are on good social terms, but not intimate. When
did you last see Miss Delia Cathcart?"

"I went to tea at the Grange . . . let me see, when was it? Time means so little to me. I can always remember *what* happened, but never *when*. I ought to remember because I had a silly fainting fit, and I had to go and lie down in Delia Cathcart's bedroom. Such an ugly room! When I felt better, it positively hurt me. Ugliness does, you know."

"Was this last week?"

"Yes, I know it was last week. I believe it was Friday. Or wasn't it? Yes, it was Friday—the day before Michael went away."

Guy didn't say, "and the day before Miss Cathcart disappeared." He said, "And would you call Miss Cathcart an attractive woman?"

"Oh, no. Not at all. Very hard and horsey. Getting on, too. The age when the soul shines through—or else it doesn't."

"Still, one never knows what people see in one another. Have you heard from your husband?"

"He left a note. You see, he had been out late at a bridge party and, when he came in, he didn't disturb me. We have separate bedrooms—so much less sordid—and I didn't find his note till after breakfast on Saturday morning. It simply said, *'Dear Gerda, I can't bear it any longer. Michael.'* What he meant by 'it,' I don't know. Michael isn't very lucid on paper. I don't know what you think of the ordinary public school education. . . ."

"Have you taken any steps to trace him?"

"No. I'm not like that. According to my ideas, that would be definitely sordid."

"Well," said Guy, "I'm afraid I shall have to be sordid. I shall have to have him traced, in case Miss Cathcart did go away with him. Did he go by car, Mrs. Willoughby?"

"Yes, to Melchester station. He left the car in a garage there—the Station Garage—and gave orders that it should be driven back here."

"That looks as if he went by train. Is there anywhere in London where he'd be likely to stay—his club, for instance?"

"He gave up his club some time ago because he used it so little. London could give him so much—art, music, drama, but he hates it. No horses, you see, Mr. Northeast. No horses."

"I must admit that on the subject of London I rather agree with him." Guy got up, but Mrs. Willoughby stayed where she was. "Oh, but, Mr. Northeast, think what London could give you. Think of the marvelous people you can meet there—painters, novelists, musicians! Think of the marvelous parties you might be invited to. . . ."

"Not me. I'm a policeman."

"Oh, well, I was thinking of myself really. You see, Mr. Northeast, I'm *intelligent*. If I were only in touch with *thinking* people. . . ."

Yet another Ancient Mariner, Guy thought, as he edged towards the door. "I'm afraid I must rush off," he said firmly. "I've a bus to catch. If you care to ring up the Melchester Police Station some time tomorrow, they may have some news of the Captain." He seized his hat from the hall chest and said, "Good afternoon, Mrs. Willoughby."

"I shan't ring up the police station," said Mrs. Willoughby behind him. "It wouldn't be like me. It would be sordid. I believe in living graciously."

Guy walked backwards down the track. "Yes," he said. "Yes. Excuse me, but the bus. . . ."

"We only pass this way once," said Mrs. Willoughby.

"That's right," said Guy, "but you must excuse me. The bus, you know . . ." He took off his hat, swung round and made off as fast as his long legs could carry him.

Walking back to Marley Green, now at the leisurely pace which his serene mind dictated, he thought about Gerda Willoughby—a foolish, emulous creature, quite tiresome enough to drive a man from home without the incentive of an affair with another woman. From what he had heard of Delia Cathcart—practical, tailor-made, hard-looking, the man of the family—he was beginning to wonder if she would fit the part of the other woman, but that was just where a psychologist would go wrong, he considered: human nature was utterly unaccountable. And why not leave it at that, he thought; why exhaust yourself tearing down roads flagged by fallacy? But he'd have to get something cut and dried, he supposed, before he faced the hardheaded Superintendent at Melchester.

He caught the bus at the Marley crossroads and, finding himself alone on the top, he took out his notebook and added to a list of names and times, his observations and impressions. The rest of the journey he spent frowning over them. Nothing fitted.

When he reached the Melchester Police Station, he saw a large old-fashioned Daimler, in charge of a chauffeur with coachman's face, drawn up by the curb, and the young constable on duty informed him in a hoarse whisper that Major Carruthers was with the Superintendent. In the starkly furnished office which smelled of yellow soap, Guy found a tall, red-faced, gray-headed man standing with his back to the empty grate. He held out his hand, said in a voice calculated to carry across a parade ground, "Ah, here's the expert," and wrung Guy's fingers in a grip of iron.

Guy said, "Good morning, I mean good evening, sir," and the Superintendent put in, as you might have known he would, "Well, young man, have you solved our problem for us?"

"I hope to God you have," roared the Chief Constable. "That Cathcart woman's been on to me again. Sorry for her and all that, what? But she rings me up every five minutes. Incidentally, Northeast—that's the name, isn't it?—as a farmer, I'd sooner have Southwest, what?—incidentally, she doesn't think much of you. Says you don't look sharp."

"She's rather an impatient lady, sir," Guy retaliated. "And I think she's been reading detective novels: she asked what deductions I'd made before I'd been in the house ten minutes. Her own theory is that Miss Cathcart's been the victim of foul play of some sort."

"Then how does she explain the suitcase? It *is* Miss Cathcart's, I suppose?" asked Dawes.

"Yes, sir. Both the sisters have identified it. Mrs. Cathcart thinks her daughter was lured away. Miss Sheila also favors the foul play theory, but suspects tramps—in particular the one whom Miss Nancy saw—or a maniac. She doesn't attempt to explain why her sister packed a bag and presumably traveled to London." He turned to the Superintendent. "Did you get any information at the station, sir?"

"I did," said Dawes. "One of the ticket collectors thinks he remembers a lady in a blue dress carrying a rawhide suitcase. She hurried up the steps, but she was in quite good time for the slow train to London—11:35."

"If he's positive," said Guy, "that disposes of Miss Sheila's theory."

"In my opinion," said the Superintendent, "it pretty well settles the whole affair. Captain Willoughby left his home the same morning. . . ."

"Can't quite see it," interrupted the Chief Constable. "Shouldn't have thought that Delia Cathcart was in Willoughby's line of country. A little bit of fluff, now . . . ?"

"Captain Willoughby left home by car early on Saturday morning; he may have arranged to pick up Miss Cathcart," said Guy. "I have seen Mrs. Willoughby and she tells me that he left a note saying that he couldn't bear it any longer, 'it' being his wife, I suppose."

"Trying woman, what?"

"I found her very trying, sir. The Captain left his car at the station garage, arranging for it to be driven back to his home. We'd better enquire what time that was, and also if Miss Cathcart was with him then. I daresay that after they had garaged the car, they went out and got breakfast, but why they should have hung about Melchester waiting for a slow train at 11:35 I've no idea. It also seems to me mighty odd that they didn't travel together. I gather that the ticket collector would have mentioned if the lady had been accompanied by a gentleman?"

"Yes," said Dawes. "I investigated that. I couldn't find anyone at the station who remembers seeing Willoughby, but of course he's not been very long in the district, so they might not know him by name. But that's neither here nor there. Wouldn't they travel separately to avoid scandal?"

"Can't avoid scandal when you run off with a woman. Got to go through it sooner or later, what? Besides they'd want to hold hands."

"I'm inclined to agree with you, sir," said Guy and the glance that Dawes shot at him said, sucking up, are you? "But that's merely a detail. Actually, the Superintendent's theory is supported by village gossip and by Miss Nancy Cathcart, who seems to have a romantic mind. Personally, I'm betting against a love affair. In the first place, I can't see a woman going off with a man without packing more frills and furbelows; in the second place, I can't see her leaving the few things she did pack in the train and not making the slightest effort to claim them."

"Perhaps she was cutting it fine or didn't want to attract attention. She may have decided to sting her young man for a complete new trousseau in Paree."

Obviously there was no moving Dawes. Guy said, "Well, let's leave that for a moment, sir, and consider another possibility. Loss of memory. That would account for the small quantity of clothes she packed, the time she wasted in Melchester and her leaving the suitcase in the railway carriage and just wandering away."

"Whoa there!" shouted the Chief Constable. "Delia Cathcart's as hard as nails—doesn't know the meaning of nerves."

"You can never tell what's in another person's mind, sir. She may have bottled things up all her life and cracked suddenly."

"But if she was wandering about London, wouldn't your people have found her by now?" asked Dawes.

"London's an easy place to hide in," said Guy, ignoring the attack. "And, of course, she may have gone further than London. She cashed a check last week. But wherever she went, with no luggage and in a queer state of mind, you'd have thought she'd have attracted attention."

Dawes frowned.

"We shall never get anywhere like this—setting up theories and then knocking them down. . . ."

"You *are* being a bit destructive, Northeast," agreed the Chief Constable. "Can't be foul play, because of the lady getting up and packing her box. Can't be loss of memory because she'd have been found by now. Can't be a love affair because she'd have packed more frills. Now let's hear you do a bit of constructing, what?"

Guy disliked nothing so much as being pushed along. He deplored the magic, which, fed on fiction and the press, has attached itself to the name of Scotland Yard. He considered that a long steady pull took you up the hill much better than a series of spectacular dashes. Gently did it, but no sooner was the name of Scotland Yard mentioned, than people expected you to produce some obscure information acquired on travels that a policeman's pay couldn't run to, or a piece of scientific knowledge never included in the curriculum of a grammar school, which would instantly solve their problem. Well, one could only do one's best. . . . He said, "I realize that I haven't got very far yet, sir. But I have a hunch that there's more in this than we realize at present. When Miss Cathcart went out to bed in the garden, she was wearing pajamas and a woolen dressing gown. In her suitcase are a silk dressing gown and a clean pair of pajamas."

"When did the laundry go?" asked Dawes.

"On Friday, the day before the disappearance. The dirty clothes basket, or soiled linen basket, or whatever you prefer to call it, in her bedroom contains two handkerchiefs. Where are the pajamas that Miss Cathcart wore that night?"

"H'm," said Dawes, compressing his lips as if determined not to say, I overlooked that.

"And where," Guy went on, "is her dressing gown? It's not in her room and there's nowhere else where she's accustomed to hang things. It strikes me as very odd, sir, that those two garments should be missing."

"Well, Dawes, what do you say to that?" asked the Chief Constable.

The Superintendent scratched his chin. "Well, sir, from the start I rather pooh-poohed the idea that she was wandering about in her nightclothes, and then the discovery of the suitcase bore out my theory; and, of course, I haven't had the opportunity of checking through the young lady's wardrobe and comparing it with the contents of the suitcase. In fact, it's a new one on me," he concluded, rather lamely.

Guy said, "I've compared the list the Super made from information received from the family with the contents of the suitcase and the only discrepancies are, one printed silk dress, one navy hat and one pair of blue suede shoes. I think we may assume that she was wearing these."

"The ticket collector remembers a lady in blue," said Dawes. "So that's OK."

"But what about . . . er . . . undergarments?" asked the Chief Constable.

"There were quite a number of sets in her room, too many for a convincing check. Mayn't we regard them as immaterial?"

"Yes, that about describes ladies' wear, these days."

"We can assume then that Miss Cathcart went away in a blue outfit, but where are the pajamas and the woolen dressing gown?"

Dawes began to doodle. He drew capital letters and embellished them with flourishes reminiscent of old-fashioned copy books. The Chief Constable cleared his throat and rattled his keys. In the end, the Chief Constable was the bravest. He said, "It beats me."

"Then what," asked Guy, "becomes of our theories? If it wasn't for the dressing gown and pajamas we could assume either loss of memory or a love affair and base our next step on the supposition that the lady was either wandering or making whoopee in town. If it wasn't for the blue outfit and the suitcase, we could begin interviewing possible suspects or dragging the local ponds."

Dawes said, "I must say, Northeast, I think you're attaching too much importance to this dressing gown. She may have had a small case or even a brown paper parcel, which she didn't leave on the rack. Miss Cathcart was seen traveling to London and her suitcase was found there. Obviously our next step is to trace her movements at, and after she left, Waterloo."

"The Yard will do that, sir. They were to ring me here at six unless I rang them first." He turned to the Chief Constable. "You, sir, said that Miss Cathcart was 'as hard as nails.' Do you consider that she is hard enough to have gone away and stayed away without sending a word to her mother?"

"'Pon my word, I don't. These Cathcarts are a very devoted family."

Dawes said, "Then what?"

"That's for you to say, sir," said Guy, turning to the Chief Constable. "They can get on with the routine enquiries in town without me."

"Meaning you're prepared to stay here? Well, aren't we all rather making a mountain out of a molehill?" He lapsed into thoughtful silence: then, at last, "All right, Northeast, if you're sure we're not wasting your time. It will keep Mrs. Cathcart quiet. Now, before I rush off, what's the program?"

"I'd rather like to have a go at the servants, always supposing the Superintendent can arrange for enquiries to be made at the station garage, hotels and places where she, or the pair of them, can have had breakfast and, of course, at the bank. It's very important to know how much money she carried."

"Can you see to that, Dawes?"

"Yes, sir, in the morning. But," he added invincibly, "always provided Captain Willoughby hasn't been traced."

As he spoke the telephone bell rang. He lifted the receiver. "London; Superintendent Hannay for you, Northeast," he said, and handed it to Guy.

Guy did most of the talking. There seemed to be more in this case, he said, than either he or Superintendent Hannay had thought likely. Major Carruthers, the Chief Constable, who was in the room with him now, had agreed to his staying on and continuing his investigations at least for a day or two. Foul play? Well, he couldn't say yet. Suicide? Well, at present nothing pointed in that direction. What he wanted eliminated was the chance that the lady was in London suffering from loss of memory or in the company of a certain Captain Willoughby. He gave details of times and trains and then turned to the Chief Constable to ask for a description of Willoughby. "Little foxy feller," said the Major and stuck. "Reddish hair, brown eyes, clean-shaven except for a small reddish mustache; age round about forty," snapped the Superintendent.

Guy spoke for a few moments longer, tactfully suggesting that some enquiries might be made at the Passport Office and then, after a polite hope that Superintendent Hannay's sciatica was better, he put down the receiver. "They'll ring you up as soon as they've any news, sir," he said to Dawes. "There shouldn't be much difficulty about tracing Willoughby. I mean, he'll have done what you'd expect—behaved in a normal manner. Same applies to Miss Cathcart, if she's with him, but of course if she's queer in the head, she may have done anything."

"You're a worrying sort of fellow, aren't you?" grumbled the Chief Constable. "Determined to spoil my night's rest with thoughts of foul play. Well, we must hope for the best, what? I must be off now—got to dress myself up for a party. Keep in touch with me, you fellers, and you, Northeast, do your best to calm down the old lady."

He strode out to his Daimler. Guy collected his suitcase and made his way through the airless streets to the Red Lion, recommended by Dawes. It was a red brick Georgian building, gay with window boxes, but inside it was less inviting: long, chilly corridors, smelling of boiled cabbage, and a labyrinth of staircases and landings piled with laundry baskets, disused hip baths and spotted mirrors, led to the cheaper bedrooms. He washed in lukewarm water, ate a lukewarm dinner, sat in a lounge among dusty palms and long-unemptied ashtrays and failed to solve the detective problem presented in a day-before-yesterday's picture paper. Dreams did not normally disturb his night's rest, but cabinet pudding, which had followed soup apparently distilled from stewed dishcloths, a fillet from one of the least appetizing of the denizens of the deep, concealed under a mound of cornflour, and veal, accompanied by ancestral peas and over-boiled potatoes, weighed heavily on his digestion. He dreamed that he was sleeping with Delia Cathcart, who wore a printed silk dress and a navy hat and shoes and kept him awake by continually getting up and searching under the bed for her woolen dressing gown.

THURSDAY

"ARE YOU AWAKE, darling?"

The old yellow face turned on the pillow.

"I haven't slept at all. How can I sleep? I suppose there's no news, darling?"

"No. I've got your letters. There's one from Aunt Alice—otherwise they're all circulars."

"Oh—the post's been. What's the time, darling?"

"Nine o'clock," said Sheila, pulling back the curtains.

"Nine o'clock!" Mrs. Cathcart sat up. "Then it's not too early to telephone to Major Carruthers."

"I shouldn't bother him yet, darling," said Sheila. "I shouldn't really. He seemed rather cross when I telephoned last night. He said that everything was in the hands of Scotland Yard now, and we should hear as soon as there was the tiniest scrap of news about our darling. There's the front door bell now. Shall I run down and see if it's anything?"

"Yes, please. And leave the door ajar. And you might tell Elspeth that I don't want anything but a little tea and toast for my breakfast."

From the top of the stairs Sheila heard a man's voice asking if he might speak to Mrs. Cathcart or one of the Miss Cathcarts. Yes, Detective-Inspector Northeast. While Sheila hesitated, Nancy came out of the dining room.

"Oh—good morning."

"Good morning, Miss Cathcart. I hope I'm not too early."

"Not a bit," said Nancy. "Have you any news for us?"

"Not yet, but I hope it won't be long now—I've got things moving.

79

What I want to do this morning is to interview all the servants here—
would that be possible?"

"I should think so," said Nancy, and, with the childish helpless-
ness that you might have found irritating or pathetic, "I don't
know . . . . I mean, I wonder how we could manage it? I'll ask my
sister. Sheila! Darling!"

Sheila revealed herself. "Oh—good morning."

"Good morning," said Guy. "I was just telling your sister that I
want to interview the servants. Tiresome, I know, but it's a routine
matter. Could I park myself somewhere and have them in one by
one? I shall only keep each of them about ten minutes."

"The drawing room would be best," said Sheila, leading the way
there. "I suppose they'll all give notice now. They'll be dreadfully
offended."

"I'll try to be tactful," said Guy, walking over to the writing table.
"When you speak to them, you might make it clear that I'm only
asking them to help me."

"Be careful with Cook, won't you?" implored Sheila. "I'll send
her first. Her name's Mrs. Hemmings. She's a widow."

By the time that Mrs. Hemmings had taken off her apron and
unexpectedly remarked that she wasn't like some, what might take
offense; she was better educated, Guy had settled himself at the writing table, opened his notebook, sharpened his pencil and written at
the top of a page, *Cook. Mrs. Hemmings. Widow.* When Mrs. Hemmings
came into the room, he wished her good morning and pointed out
that as the most important member of the staff and the one with the
widest experience of life, she was the best equipped to help him.
Mrs. Hemmings agreed. What did these bits of girls know? she asked,
tossing her prim head; she could tell him some tales of kitchenmaids
she'd had under her—they could read, all right, but whatever was
the use of that when they couldn't make no sense out of what they
were reading? Poor dates! But Mrs. Hemmings wasn't like some.

If she could help Guy in any way, she would do so to the best of
her ability.

Guy, drawing setting suns on Mrs. Cathcart's blotting paper,
wanted to know what Mrs. Hemmings really thought about this affair
of Miss Delia. Before she disappeared, had she seemed worried or
unhappy about anything?

"That's what's got me puzzled, sir. We know what old maids are,
especially at the time when they gives up 'ope, but Miss Delia, she's
always busy and 'appy over them 'orses of 'ers. And very devoted to

'er mother and sisters she is—sees to everything for them. Speaking for ourselves, we finds 'er a bit too managing for our tastes, but that's another thing altogether."

"She isn't liked by the staff?"

"No. She's fair, I'll say that for 'er, but she's sharp. Young Ames, he calls 'er 'The Sergeant Major,' and though I don't 'old with speaking disrespectful of anybody, he's about right there. Miss Sheila, she's well enough, but she isn't one you could take to. Doesn't speak much. Proud, that's what she is. The girls like Miss Nancy best. She doesn't interfere with nobody and many's the kindness she's done unbeknownst."

"Yes," said Guy. "That's more or less how I summed them up. And about this row Miss Delia had with the kitchenmaid?"

"She isn't kitchenmaid, sir. They don't run to that. Jessie's between me and Elspeth, and a better girl for work I never come across."

"Good-tempered sort of a girl, is she?"

"That's right. 'Appy-go-lucky kind of kid. I've known 'er flare up, but it's all over in a minute, and then it's done and done with."

"And Albert Funge?"

"E's all right. Bit of a socialist 'e is, always down on the gentry, and I can't deny that 'e's been one for the girls. But as I said to Mrs. Cathcart, very often that sort makes the best 'usbins once they settles down."

Guy then asked her to cast her mind back to Friday night: did she remember anything out of the ordinary—any absurd, trivial little thing. Mrs. Hemmings couldn't say that she did; she'd been tired; her legs ached awful; and she'd gone up to bed along with Elspeth and Taylor, who always went early, leaving the door unlocked for Jessie, which she freely owned that strictly speaking she shouldn't of done. Her room was at the other end of the house, over Mrs. Cathcart's, and she hadn't heard Jessie come in or Miss Delia and Albert going on.

Guy persevered.

"Did you fall asleep at once?"

"No, that I didn't. My legs was aching. I remember I lay and wondered what 'appened to a person when their veins burst. And then I began to think about my poor Aunt Beat."

"What happened to her?"

"She 'ad an ulcer on 'er leg and they took 'er off to the Melchester Cottage 'Orspital and there she passed away. I've got an 'orror of 'orspitals. Well, I lay and thought about 'orspitals and then I began to think about a savory out of the paper, what Miss Delia wanted me to try."

"Was your window open?"

"Yes, it was. I know that, because I 'ad 'arf a mind not to open it. Sometimes the owls 'oot 'orrible in the fir trees in the drive. Oh . . . !"

"Yes?"

"It's nothing much, but now I come to think of it, I did 'ear a whistle. Sort of catcall it was—like this: phi-phew. I remember thinking it was them damned owls tuning up, and then I thought, no; it's a person. I reckon it was some of them bits of lads out in the lane."

"What time was this?"

"That I can't tell you, sir."

"Well," said Guy, "it sounds as though there was someone about anyway." He knew it was useless to ask her to keep anything to herself, so he added, "You see, I'm anxious to find someone who might have seen Miss Delia going away. But of course that would have been much too early."

"Oh, yes," agreed Mrs. Hemmings. "I heard the 'all clock chime eleven, but not twelve."

Guy asked her a few more questions—merely routine ones, he said—where her home was and where she had been working before she came to the Grange. Then he thanked her effusively and asked her to send Jessie in.

Jessie came pop-eyed, a startled robin, and for a few moments Guy talked reassuringly about her home, which, it transpired, was three miles away at Little Hitherford. They discussed the motion of the Little Hitherford bus—it reminded Jessie of a trip round the bay, which she had taken during her holiday last year—and then Guy said that he wanted her to help him: his idea about Miss Delia Cathcart was that the poor thing was suffering from loss of memory, and he was hoping very much to find someone who had seen or heard her after she had gone out of the house on Friday night. It seemed rather funny to him that, after their unsatisfactory parting under Miss Delia's eye, Jessie's young gentleman hadn't come back to say good night properly. "That's what I should have done," he said, trying to produce an admiring glance, but suspecting that he had only achieved a leer.

Jessie stood up for Funge.

"I daresay he would of, only Miss Delia was sleeping in the garden and she's got such sharp cars. Besides, it's not very nice and Albert wouldn't want to get mix-muddled-up with any goings on."

"What goings on?"

Jessie colored.

"Well, I shouldn't like to say. The gentry are down enough on us for anything, but they're not so particular themselves. If I took a fancy for sleeping out in the garden, it 'ud be, 'Really, Jessie, what are you thinking of?'" She imitated a voice which Guy supposed was Delia's.

"Well," he said with a friendly smile, "you see, Miss Delia is a little bit older than you are."

"That makes no difference," declared Jessie, looking worldly-wise. "Miss Delia's no more than a year younger than our Mum, but she's man-mad, that's what she is. You mark my words, sir, there's a man at the back of this affair."

Guy was a little surprised at her volubility. He had expected her to be shy, possibly struck dumb. Then he remembered how chatty Albert Funge had been, the long words he had attempted, his brisk assertion that had he seen or heard anything unusual he would have notified the police. Perhaps Albert had passed on to his young woman some of his own deplorable cocksureness. Guy proceeded to make the best of it.

"Yes," he said. "Other people have hinted at that. But I expect you can help me more than they did. Which of Miss Delia's friends would you bet on?"

"It's not only her friends," said Jessie. "I know she rides about a lot with that Captain Willoughby. If I was his wife, I'd give her something. But you don't want only to look among the gentry."

"Oh? Then, who?"

"I'm naming no names," said Jessie, "nor making no accusations. But hours and hours they've been shut up together in the stable."

"Oh, I see," said Guy. "Thank you for the hint. It's a relief to meet someone who doesn't go about with their eyes shut." Nasty little beast, he thought, and wasn't at all sorry to say, "By the way, did Mrs. Cathcart give you permission to go into Melchester on Saturday morning?"

"I didn't ask for permission," said Jessie, tossing her head. "I told Cook I was going and she said, 'Please yourself, girl,' that's what she said."

"I see. Speaking for myself I'm glad you went because you may have seen something—any little thing—that might help me. Did you pass the station?"

"No, I didn't. Mr. Funge set me down at the Statue, and I went to the registry office."

"Which one?"

"Mrs. Whittamore. That's the best class. The other is only for generals and suchlike. Mrs. Whittamore's sent me over twenty places already."

"Good. And afterwards?"

"Afterwards Albert met me at the Cosy Cafe. We 'ad coffee and iced cakes. It's ever so nice there."

"And you didn't see any sign of Miss Delia or any friend of hers?"

"No. The only person I saw was Lady Angela from the 'All. Oh, she did look a picture! 'Ad a little 'at on 'er 'ead—like a tomtit on a round of beef, it was."

"And on the way there and back you saw no one you knew, no car you recognized?"

"No, sir. I'd say if I 'ad. I've nothink to 'ide," said Jessie.

"Pity," said Guy, and then, "Now I want to go back to Friday night. After you'd finished rowing with Miss Delia and you had got up to your bedroom, did you go straight to bed?"

"No, sir, I didn't. I went into Elspeth's room and we talked it over. She's a nice girl, she is. She'd got 'old of 'arf a dish of cauliflower-oh-grating and saved it for me."

"Oh well, girls will be girls. How long did you stay talking?"

"Not over ten minutes."

"And then, I suppose, you went to your bedroom. Whereabouts is it?"

"It's the attic over Miss Delia's room. But I didn't 'ear anythink."

"Was the window open?"

"Oh, you mean anythink going on outside?" For the first time the cheeky face clouded. "No, I didn't."

"Did you look out—to see the last of your young man or to wave good night to him?"

"No, I didn't. 'E'd been gone ten minutes. 'E told me next morning that 'e went straight 'ome and got in sharp at eleven."

"And you didn't hear anyone about when you opened your window?"

"I didn't open my winder. Miss Delia's always on at us to sleep with them open, but our Mum says that the night air's un'ealthy."

"I see. Well, Jessie, that's all and I hope you'll find a place that will suit you. By the way, where were you before you came here?"

"I was scullerymaid at the 'All. Left to better myself. 'Er Ladyship," said Jessie defiantly, "give me a good character."

Guy sent her away with a message to the effect that he would like to see the housemaid next, and, while he was waiting, he made a few entries in his notebook. Elspeth, instead of bouncing in as Jessie had done, came in slowly and quietly. She was a very pretty girl in her middle twenties. She had curly fair hair gathered in a loose knot and clear gray eyes under finely penciled brows. There was none of Jessie's alertness about her, but an air of calm, almost gracious, maturity.

She gave her name as Elspeth Barlow and she answered Guy's questions briefly and thoughtfully. She had noticed nothing strange about Miss Delia. Yes, she was a managing type, but after all, someone had to take the lead in a family. She had men friends, but why not? Queen Victoria was dead and England wasn't Turkey. No, on Friday night she hadn't seen or heard anything. Her window had been open top and bottom, but her room was on the south side of the house and looked over the paddock. Yes, she had kept the remains of a dish of cauliflower-au-gratin for Jessie, who was always hungry, and as the kid had seemed a little upset over her row with Miss Delia, she had stayed up for about ten minutes talking to her. No, she wasn't particularly fond of Jessie, but the child came from a poor home; she was an honest sort of kid, but Albert Funge wasn't doing her any good with his pretentious ideas and half-baked socialism.

"I wonder if you'll excuse me making rather a personal remark," said Guy presently. "What puzzles me is that you seem so much better educated than the other girls here. If I'd met you outside the place, I should never have guessed that you were in domestic service."

Now the serene gray eyes looked troubled, but Elspeth said, "You're making a mistake, sir. I'm no different."

"You speak differently."

"Oh, well, I daresay I do. You see, Mother married a bit beneath her. And Father wasn't quite . . . well, he was in a better position than say Jessie's father. He was a gamekeeper."

"I see," said Guy, almost sure that she was lying. "And you've always been in service?"

"Ever since I was fourteen," said Elspeth with unnecessary firmness.

"And where were you before you came to Mrs. Cathcart?"

"In London with a Mr. and Mrs. Johnson. They went back to America."

"Oh. And before that?"

"I was with them for several years. Before that, I was with a lady who was a widow. She's dead now."

"Then when you came here, I suppose it was these Johnsons who gave you a reference?"

"Well, they didn't actually," said Elspeth and her right hand went to her left as if to twist nervously a ring that she had been used to wearing on her third finger. "Unfortunately for me, they had already gone back to America. They left me a written reference, but I'd sent it to a lady and she never returned it. But Mrs. Cathcart wanted a housemaid urgently and I saw Miss Delia and she said she was a judge of character and engaged me."

Guy's blue eyes always looked a little blank, but scarcely anything escaped them. He had noticed the movement of her hands and now he said, "Are you married?"

Elspeth gave a gasp. "Good gracious no. What on earth makes you think so?"

It wasn't well done. It wouldn't have deceived anyone. But there it was. With a laugh, which sounded rather false to him, he said, "Oh, I don't know. Somehow, you give that impression," and he went on to discuss the subject of Delia's clothes; if she had been starting off in a hurry, where would she be likely to hang up, or throw down, her woolen dressing gown?

"Oh, she would never throw anything down," said Elspeth, looking happier. "She's very tidy. She always hangs that dressing gown in her wardrobe; there's a hook on the back of the door, but she won't have anything there but her hunting crop. And I don't think that in any circumstances she would have taken that old woolen thing with her. She only used it when she slept in the garden."

There were other questions which Guy wanted to ask, but they were personal ones and on the subject of her own affairs, this angelic looking creature was not, he considered, to be relied upon. He dismissed her, and almost immediately the immaculate and efficient Taylor walked briskly in.

"Good morning, sir," said Taylor, although it was she who had opened the front door to him. "A fine day again! I don't know as I can help you, but I'll try all I can. I've nothing to 'ide. My name's Patricia Gwendoline Taylor, aged twenty-eight, and I'm parlormaid here. I came with a good reference from the Honorable Mrs. Sprott."

"Thank you," said Guy. "Now, Miss Taylor, what is your own private opinion about this affair?"

Taylor studied her nails—a virginal occupation, Guy thought, not like that telltale twisting of a recently discarded ring.

"If you'll excuse my mentioning such a thing, sir, I should say that there was a member of the stronger sex involved. I'm engaged to be married myself, so I understands these things."

"You mean—a married man?"

"Well, that I can't say. Either a married man or one in a different walk of life—any'ow someone of whom her mother wouldn't approve."

"Have you any facts to give me, or is this only an idea?"

"It's not a very nice thing to say," replied Taylor, "but, in a way of her own, Miss Delia is one for the men. She 'asn't got no 'it,' I grant you, but she talks about sports and games and gets off that way. She likes young men about the place, too. In my belief, it was that that made her sack her old groom and take on that iggerant young Ames. She's always out on 'orseback with him or in the stables, and she's always giving 'im presents. 'Is wife don't care for it, and I don't blame 'er."

Servants' gossip, of course. If Guy won a football pool or rose to be Chief Commissioner, he was damned if he'd keep any. Could there be smoke without fire? But what a poor fire! Ames had got home at three o'clock, and Delia had left the Grange before seven and taken the 11:35

"All the same," he said, "I don't see how Ames could have upset Miss Delia—you know, my own opinion is that she's suffering from loss of memory. Now, Miss Taylor, while you waited at table, did you ever hear any criticism of Miss Delia from the rest of the family?"

No, Taylor had never heard any words pass. Very fond of each other the four ladies were—darling this and darling that—in Taylor's opinion, it was soppy. On the Friday night she had gone to sleep as soon as her head had touched the pillow. Her room was next to Elspeth's, on the south side of the house and even if she had been awake, she wouldn't have heard anything.

So Taylor went away—to get on, she said, with her silver, and, after writing up his notebook, Guy rose and stretched himself. He must look into this unsavory gossip about Ames, and he must delve into the past of poor pretty Elspeth. In the meantime, a nose-round was indicated.

For everything was still so damnably vague. Go on and ferret out that Delia and her groom were lovers, that Elspeth was married and had six children, that Funge had hung round the Grange till midnight whistling; and where were you? Delia Cathcart had walked through the barrier on the up side platform at Melchester Station in good time for the train at 11:35, and there wasn't a scrap of evidence to show that any harm had come to her. The only thing to do when a case got into a state like this was, he considered, to empty your mind of your theories, shut your eyes and open your mouth and see what Father Christmas would give you.

He went out of the front door into the blazing sunshine. Well, of course, it hadn't been like this when Delia Cathcart, in her striped pajamas and woolen dressing gown, had gone out to sleep on the lawn. Then there had been utter darkness under the tall hedges, moonshine across the glaring gravel and on the lawn. Supposing that someone standing under the hedge had whistled to Delia? She would have got up and gone across the lawn to him and they would have stood in the shadow talking, making plans. "I'll pick you up soon after seven tomorrow morning," Willoughby would have said. "If I leave it till later, my wife will have a thousand and one questions to ask. And let's waste hours of time dawdling about dear old Melchester," he must have said, "and then we can catch a nice slow train that stops at all the stations. And I don't like that old woolen dressing gown of yours," he must have said, "or those pink striped pajamas; when you take them off be sure to hide them—bury them or burn them or wrap them round a stone and throw them into a duck pond." It was odd how a matter-of-fact fellow like Dawes could support such a theory; but perhaps it wouldn't have occurred to him to reconstruct the insane conversation, which, if he were right, must have passed between Delia and Captain Willoughby.

And supposing Ames had been the whistler? The middle of the moonlit lawn was rather an exposed spot for a necking party; again, Delia would have risen from her bed and met him in the shadow of a building or a hedge. A less tidy garden might have told tales, but this damnable lawn was mowed and rolled till it looked like a billiard table and a backbreaking survey of the roots of the hedges yielded nothing.

Wondering what sort of a fool he must have looked to the maids, whose caps, as he rose from all-fours, bobbed away from the windows, Guy straightened his back and abandoning the lawn walked out of the wicket gate and towards the stable. Flavia's loose box was empty and Ames was nowhere to be seen, so it was to be assumed that he was out exercising her.

Seizing this heaven-sent opportunity, Guy walked into the forage room and into the harness room that opened out of it. Ames smoked Park Drives, read John Bull and was an indifferent tack cleaner. He collected cigarette cards, followed greyhound racing, and took more pride than you would have guessed in his personal appearance. That was all.

Guy came out into the sunshine. The messy bit of ground at the side of the stable was quite a relief from the rather suburban tidiness of the rest of the property. Here were ladders, an old hen coop, the garden roller, and the midden was piled high against the wall of the stable. There was good stuff at the bottom of it, the countryman observed, but the top argued sinful extravagance; for some time—probably since the old groom had left—an unnecessary amount of straw had been taken from the manure out of the loose boxes. Ames was extravagant and—*vide* Taylor and Jessie—Delia had been too infatuated to check him.

Well, this piece of ground wasn't a romantic meeting place, but it was a good place to hang about: you could approach by Lovers' Lane, walk in at the five barred gate and slip up the back drive into the shadow of the shrubbery. Tired after your day's work, you would lean against the stable wall, smoke a cigarette and throw the fag end on the midden. But that was five days ago! With one horse stabled, at least ten barrow loads had been piled on since then, and Ames had probably pitched dozens and dozens of cigarette ends there as he went backwards and forwards on his lawful occasions.

Then Guy, looking at the midden, saw something which might have escaped the eye of a sharper man. Above the heap, the usual cloud of tiny flies was swarming, but, crawling up the stable wall, circling round, returning and crawling back into the straw, were half a dozen large lazy blowflies. There shouldn't have been anything in the midden to attract blowflies; no gentleman's groom or gardener but only the most untidy negligent people would throw a carcass there. But perhaps it was a dead rat or a sparrow. Guy took a pitchfork, which was against the wall, mounted the heap and began to turn the straw over.

The first he saw of Delia Cathcart was her hand with a gold signet ring on it and the sleeve of her brownish woolen dressing gown. He wasn't squeamish, but in the sunshine, with the fantails cooing, it was rather horrible, and he stopped forking while his stomach settled. Then, with more caution, he set to work removing the top layers and, when he had used his hands to scoop away the manure, which had dropped through his pitchfork, there she lay with open eyes, blankly gazing at him. Rigor mortis had long passed; she lay limply with her arms outstretched, as though crucified.

Guy got down from the midden and went quickly through the yard into the harness room. There he found a horse rug, which he took back and laid over the body. Then he walked up the drive to the house. The front door stood open and, as he passed through the hall, he could hear voices in the drawing room.

He knocked at the door, and was told to come in. Sheila, at the piano, was poring over a page of music; Nancy, seated on the sofa, was darning a stocking.

He said, "I wonder if I might telephone?"

Sheila said, "Oh, certainly," but neither she nor her sister moved, and he had to say, "Could I have the room to myself for a minute?"

"Oh—I'm sorry," stammered Sheila. "Come along, Nancy. We'll camp in the dining room, shall we, darling?"

Nancy gathered her things together with exasperating slowness, and Sheila, picking up *The Times.*, turned over a vase of flowers and cried out that she must fetch a cloth and mop up the water. Guy said his handkerchief would do, sacrificed a clean one, and at last got quit of them. Then, on thorns lest Ames should return to the stable in his absence, he made haste to call the Melchester Police Station.

"Northeast speaking. I say, sir . . ."

"Oh, it's you, is it?" said the Superintendent. "Want to know if the Yard have rung you up? Well, they haven't. I must say they're taking their time. . . ."

"It wasn't that. It was to tell you that I've just found Miss Cathcart's body."

"Good lord! Where?"

"At the Grange. Buried in the midden, sir. Will you come along with the whole boiling? You'll attract less attention if you turn up Lovers' Lane and come in the back way. Now, I must get back. I don't like leaving the body."

He jammed down the receiver and tiptoed across the room, anxious not to be delayed by questions from Sheila or Nancy. As he passed through the hall, the dining-room door opened and Sheila's voice behind him said, "Oh—Mr. Northeast . . ." but he ignored her and, listening tensely for the sound of hoofs, hurried back to the stable.

The yard, as before, was deserted. On the brown roof the fantails cooed; a pair of them, flying across to the fir trees, broke the silence with the sound of wings, and their blue shadows swept across the cobbles. Beyond the yew hedges and the lawn the white house stood solid and comfortable; Delia Cathcart had had most things— money in her pocket, country life, the affection of her family, good living, servants to wait on her, horses in her stable—what had gone wrong that someone had so hated her? Well, say she'd missed love and, because she'd been too stupid to see that life's only a chapter, she'd snatched and grabbed, thinking that was the way to gather roses. Into whose garden had she trespassed? Gerda Willoughby's? That *poseuse* could kid herself into anything. Haggard Mrs. Ames's? Was it a woman's crime anyway?

* * * *

A car hooted. Guy hurried down the back drive to the gate. Dawes climbed out of the small blue police car. His jaw was thrust forward. He looked stern, determined and in charge.

"I've brought a couple of constables," he snapped, indicating the huge figures clambering out of the car with difficulty. "The fingerprint man and the photographer are just behind. Ambulance on its way. Doctor Baker should be here, and I've phoned the Chief Constable. Where's the body?"

"This way," said Guy and led him to the midden.

"Well," said Dawes, looking unmoved on the limp body, "that settles it. We know what we're up against now, Inspector. Murder!"

Guy was unreasonably irritated. He said, "Or manslaughter."

"Oh, naturally," said Dawes, "but not loss of memory. Hullo, that sounds like Doctor Baker."

The police surgeon was a little man with a skipping step and a fussy manner. Shepherded by one of the outsize constables, he sprang, elflike, from the laurels. "Tch, tch," he said. "Miss Delia Cathcart. I've played tennis with her."

He skipped over to the midden and began a quick examination, chirping, "Tch, tch," and, "Dear me, dear me," and "A bad business!" Then, "Bluntish instrument," he said, "but with an edge to it— I'd say a hatchet that needed sharpening. One blow, struck slightly from above, and she died at once. Oh yes, oh yes, a blunt hatchet."

Guy asked, "And when. . . ?"

"Can't tell you that, my dear man. Much too late to give more than a guess, and guessing doesn't help anybody."

"But very roughly. . . ."

"She's been dead four or five days."

"She was missed on Saturday morning," said Guy, "and she was last seen by her family on Friday evening, but there's some evidence that she was alive at eleven-thirty on Saturday."

"Can't confirm that," said the doctor. "Can't deny it, either. Sorry, can't help you. Delia Cathcart. Dear me, dear me. A bad business."

His last words were drowned by a roar from the shrubbery, "Where's Dawes? Where's Northeast? Come along, man, move to it!" and, followed by a beetroot-faced constable, the Chief Constable, dressed in white flannels, a dark blue jacket, a Panama hat and a regimental tie, came striding towards them.

Dawes sprang to attention. "Glad I caught you, sir," he said. "I rang you as soon as Inspector Northeast reported finding the body. There it is, sir."

"Good God," said the Chief Constable. "On the midden!"

Dawes continued: "Doctor Baker gives as the cause of death a blow from a bluntish instrument, probably a hatchet."

"Good God. And the time?"

"Four or five days ago."

"Good God, Doctor, is that all you can do for us?"

"That's all, Major. Much too late, you see. No use guessing."

The Chief Constable swung round on Guy.

"Well, Northeast, who did it?"

Guy did his best. "I picked up a lot of useful information this morning, sir. I suggest that when the body's been removed, we have a talk in the harness room. And, by the way, sir, what about breaking it to the family?"

The Chief Constable growled, "That can wait, can't it?"

"I don't think so, sir. They've only got to look out of one of the upstairs windows and they'll see the ambulance. Besides, one of the young ladies might come strolling down here."

"Good God! *That* wouldn't do. I suppose you want *me* to break it?"

"I think that would be best, sir. After all, you know them socially."

The Chief Constable made no reply but braced his shoulders and, with the look of a man who doesn't shrink from an unpleasant duty, went striding off towards the house. Acting his part, thought Guy, and wished he had one. It must be a help in life, he thought, to have a character to live up to; to be Carruthers, a soldier and a gentleman, or Dawes, a man of iron and thunder. They knew where they were, those people.

The police surgeon, skipping up to Dawes, said, "You'll want a P.M., I suppose, Superintendent?"

"Sure."

"Right. Right. I'll get through with that this evening and I'll let you have a report tonight or first thing tomorrow. I doubt if there'll be much more to tell you. Miss Delia Cathcart. Yes, yes. A bad business. Extraordinary thing to happen."

He chirped on, but above his voice Guy had caught the sound of hoofs—eager hoofs, stepping delicately down the high road. The photographers were busy with their cameras and the ambulance men were standing ready; Dawes was making some reply to the Doctor, so Guy faded off down the path and met Ames at the gate. Flavia was fussing about the cars in the Lane, and Ames, with an angry scowl on his face, was kicking her along, impatient of her affected terror. Guy spoke to the mare. She promptly lost interest in the cars and quieted down.

Guy said to Ames, "The police are in charge here now. I'd be obliged if you'd turn that mare out in the paddock."

"Can't do that," said the groom sulkily. "She's standing in by Miss Cathcart's orders."

"I told you that the police were in charge here," said Guy evenly. "Put the mare out and then you can get off to your dinner."

"I can't put her in the paddock, sir," said the groom with a change of manner. "She and Skylark will be kicking. I could put her in the orchard, here."

"That'll do."

The groom opened a gate on the left, which led into an apple orchard. He unsaddled Flavia, took off her bridle, and, as she spun round to gallop off, gave a slash with his switch at her hind quarters. It was a small thing, but Guy, who had once had his ears boxed for swishing a halter behind a pony he'd unloosed, knew at once that there was some truth in the gossip he'd listened to that morning—it wasn't for his way with horses that Ames had kept his place as groom to Miss Delia Cathcart.

"All right," he said. "You can go down the lane. I'll take the saddle and bridle."

"Anything wrong, sir?" asked Ames, shooting a quick dark glance at him.

"You'll hear presently," said Guy, and went back to the stable. He told Dawes, "The groom's gone home to his dinner. He lives in that cottage across the lane. I'd like the constable at the gate to keep an eye on it."

"The groom? Where does he come in?"

"Here and there. I shall want a talk with him presently."

"Oh well, I'll just mention it," said Dawes.

He gave a message to the constable who was standing by the shrubbery, and Guy went forward to meet the Chief Constable, who came back into the yard looking ten years older. "Very distressing," he said to Guy. "Hated the job."

Guy made a sympathetic noise and said, "How did they take it?"

"Hard. Especially little Miss Nancy. Couldn't seem to realize it. Numb. The other one seemed more prepared for it."

"She suspected something of the sort, sir. So did Mrs. Cathcart."

"I didn't like the looks of the old lady. I told those girls to ring up her doctor. It'll give them something to do, anyway. Now, Northeast, I gather you want a conference?"

"In the harness room, I thought, sir. I've sent the groom home to his dinner."

The Chief Constable bellowed "Dawes!" and Guy led the way into the harness room. Dawes stood blocking the light from the window, which looked on the orchard; the Chief Constable sat on the solitary Windsor chair, and Guy leaned against the wall with his head among the bridles.

"Fire away, Northeast," ordered the Chief Constable.

"Well, sir," Guy began, "I got here at nine o'clock this morning, and with Miss Cathcart's permission I interviewed each of the servants separately. The cook, Mrs. Hemmings, supplied me with a very suggestive piece of evidence. Her room is at the end of the house and it looks over the rose garden. On Friday night between eleven and twelve she was lying awake and she heard a whistle."

Dawes said, "Owls."

"No, sir, I don't think so. She's used to the owls. She attributed this whistle to boys in the lane, but it's quite on the cards that someone was signalling to Miss Delia."

"But who, man, who?" thundered the Chief Constable.

"I'm coming to that, sir. I then saw the between-maid. She was the one who, on Friday night, soon after ten o'clock, had a row with Miss Delia. Her young man, Albert Funge, was with her, and he joined in, and Miss Delia threatened to report him to his employer. I had previously interviewed Funge and found him an unpleasant and not wholly truthful character. However, the girl, Jessie, denies that he hung about the place, and he claims to have been back at his home by eleven. I've not had time to go into that yet, but, as a long shot, it's worth trying."

"Shouldn't bother about him," said Dawes. "There's others with much more motive."

"That's right, sir. All the same, we won't quite forget him. The girl went on to tell me—and this was later substantiated by the parlormaid—that Miss Delia was 'one for the men' and didn't confine her attentions to the 'gentry'."

"Good God," said the Chief Constable, growing redder. "A nice open-air woman like that! Nonsense. You've been listening to servants' gossip, Inspector."

"Unfortunately we have to. I'm afraid you won't like this, sir, but in the opinion of both of these girls, there was something between the groom and Miss Delia."

"I don't believe that."

"I was inclined to take it with a pinch of salt myself, but I've noticed one or two little things about Ames. He's not a good man with horses; Miss Delia lived for them, and since grooms are easy to get, she must have had some reason of her own for keeping him on. I had a talk with him the day I came down, and he told me that he had spent Friday evening at the Dog and Duck and then gone home. His wife, however, states that he didn't get in till three o'clock in the morning."

"Good God," said the Chief Constable. "That looks pretty bad. All right, Northeast, you win, though I must say I should never have thought that a woman like Delia Cathcart would have carried on with her groom."

Guy said warily, "I don't know much about these social distinctions, sir, but wasn't the Cathcart's money made in trade? The servants talk about them as 'jumped up' people. Well, isn't it three generations and back to the plow?"

"I see what you're driving at," said the Chief Constable. "Yes, the Cathcarts were biscuits, but they've been out of it for some time and this county isn't Shropshire by any means. But I see what you're driving at." He cleared his throat and tried to say, *"Nostalgie de la boue."*

"Pardon, sir?" said Dawes.

"Homesickness for the gutter," translated the Chief Constable.

"I don't see it, sir," said Dawes.

"Never mind," said the Chief Constable, and he almost winked at Guy. "Carry on, Northeast."

"There was one rather odd thing, sir, though it may have no bearing on the case at all. The housemaid, Elspeth Barton, came to Mrs. Cathcart without any references. She's much better educated than you'd expect a housemaid to be, and I'd bet a hundred to one that she's a married woman."

"Surely that's quite irrelevant," said Dawes.

"It may be, sir, but in a case like this you've got to cast the net very wide. And be thankful for even very small fish," said Guy.

"Well," said the Chief Constable, pushing back his chair, "on what you've told me, I don't mind betting that the groom is our man."

"He seems the likeliest at the moment, sir. This midden business definitely points to him. I mean, sir, would anyone else have dared to leave the body there?"

"How deep down was the body?"

"I should say I forked off about nine or ten barrowloads, sir. Ames seems to be an extravagant fellow—there was more straw there than manure. Presuming that he took out two barrowloads a day, then the murderer didn't bury the body very deep. Anybody but the groom himself took a tremendous risk—"

Dawes interrupted, "All murderers take risks, otherwise none of them would hang. He may have been in a hurry. I see him as a man who knows about stable management and so on, knows that at this time of year a muck heap isn't likely to be disturbed."

Guy said, "What that fellow Ames mucks out of a stable won't be ready for a garden for years. And not much use then. . . ."

"That's by the way," said Dawes and gathered himself together in a way that said, unless I take the lead, you'll never get anywhere. "As I was saying, our man knows country ways. He's not a tramp or a homicidal maniac or the deceased would never have come to his whistle; no, sir, he's someone she was expecting and knew well. The mistake you're making, Inspector, is this way: Ames might, if the servants' gossip is to be believed, for any of a dozen reasons, have done her in, but then, why did she pack her suitcase?"

The Superintendent paused to take breath, but the Chief Constable thought it was because he expected a reply to his question. "Yes, we've got to fit that damn suitcase in somehow. Got any theory, Northeast?"

"I don't like theorizing too soon, sir."

"I believe in having a working theory," said Dawes. "And this is how I explain things." He paused for a moment, cleared his throat, and then held forth at length.

"We'll assume that the deceased, a spinster, suffering from sex repression, was one for the men, and, though there's some that point to the groom, there's others that suggest she was carrying on with a gentleman of her own class—Captain Willoughby. Well, I look at it this way: Captain Willoughby, being a married man, comes to meet the deceased by arrangement at night, and persuades her to elope. Deceased goes indoors and packs her bag, but, at the last moment, thinking perhaps of her mother, changes her mind. Still in her dressing gown and carrying the bag, she informs the Captain of her decision. In the course of the ensuing quarrel he administers the fatal blow. Having hidden the body, he makes off with the suitcase. The next morning, he decides to get rid of this evidence, pops it into the slow train and travels by the fast one himself. And now he's sitting pretty in London."

There was a moment's pause. Then the Chief Constable said, "Well, that seems logical enough, but what about the ticket collector's evidence, Dawes?"

"The ticket collector *thinks* he saw the young lady, sir. But is he going to swear it?"

"Damn the feller! Why can't he make up his mind? All this shilly-shallying gets us nowhere. 'Pon my soul, I think I'll side with Northeast and plump for the groom."

"We've no case against anyone yet, sir," said Guy, afraid that the Chief Constable was going to ask for the handcuffs. "To my mind, we've got three obvious suspects: Ames, Willoughby, Funge; but there are others previously mentioned, whom we've rather lost sight of— the tramp, whom Miss Nancy saw, and a veterinary surgeon, who is reported to have had some sort of grudge against Miss Delia. There may be a dozen others. We've not discovered any real motive yet. What we've got to do, sir, is to eliminate; tackle all their alibis, beginning with Ames."

"That's all very well, Northeast. Alibis for when? We don't know when the murder was done," said the Chief Constable. "I'd sooner work on the personal equation. When I was in the Service I was considered a good judge of men, and I can tell you this I've met Willoughby out hunting and he's a decent feller."

Dawes said, "But perhaps a bit hasty . . . ?"

"Well . . . perhaps."

"Saw red and hit her—that's my theory, sir."

"A decent feller wouldn't hit a woman. No, Dawes, I'm backing the groom, and it's up to you to see that he's to be found when we want him."

"You can rely on me seeing to that, sir," said Dawes grimly. "But I must say I should feel happier if we could lay our hands on Willoughby."

"That's up to the Yard."

"There hasn't been much progress so far."

"If he's in London, they'll find him," said Guy with a confidence he didn't really feel. Then turning to the Chief Constable, he added: "There's a lot to be straightened out yet, sir. There's a blue outfit missing from her wardrobe and—where is her handbag, which, we have reason to believe, contained money? We can't rule out robbery yet, sir."

Dawes snorted impatiently. "Now we're off round the mulberry bush again . . . !"

The Chief Constable uttered a kind of fierce groan.

"Robbery? How much had she on her?"

"I think Superintendent Dawes was going to ascertain that, sir."

"Yes. I have the matter in hand, sir. In fact I should have been at the bank now if I hadn't been called out here."

"Well, you'd better get busy in Melchester, Dawes, and leave Northeast to ferret round here. You can come back with me and leave him your car."

"There are the two constables, sir . . . ?"

"I could use them poking round for the weapon," said Guy, ignoring the Superintendent's angry frown.

"Right! They're under your orders, Northeast. Now, it's long past my lunch time and talking hasn't got us very much further." He stopped at the door. "Murder's not nice, Northeast, but it's particularly nasty when it's one of your friends."

The Chief Constable turned and strode quickly down the drive to his car. Dawes gave the constables their orders and then hurried after his chief as fast as was compatible with his dignity.

Guy watched the car out of sight, wondering whether those two strong men would have thought more of him if he had given them the opportunity to plant their flat feet on the theories which, like mountains seen through clearing mist, were forming in his mind. Then he turned to the constables and said in his quiet voice that didn't sound as though it were giving orders, "I want you to look round and see if you can find the usual blunt instrument and a blue dress, a blue hat, a blue pair of shoes and a lady's handbag."

"Yessir. Shrubbery, duck pond and so forth . . . ?"

"That's the idea and then further afield. Why not start on the stable sump now?"

The stable drain ran out beside the midden and a sprinkling of straw lay over the broken grating which protected it. The larger of the two constables took up the pitchfork which Guy had left against the wall, and raked the straw away; then he prised up the grating, knelt down and dragging up his sleeve inserted a large red hand into the sump. He groped for a moment and then his moon-face turned to Guy. "Law lumme, got 'im in one, sir." He straightened his back and heaved himself upright. In his hand was a hatchet, dripping with malodorous slime.

THURSDAY (continued)

THE KITCHEN WINDOWS were open and the blue willow-pattern curtains swung in the light hay-scented breeze. The room was cool and
gay with bright china and shining pots and pans. Guy remembered
some of the dark disorderly kitchens into which his work had taken
him; here was order and method, a place for everything and everything in its place. It was unbelievable that in this sunny house, among
these pleasant people, a hideous cancer of perverted passion had
flourished unsuspected; there are tragedies and tragedies, and at
this moment he came near to hoping that the next few hours would
crumble his fine theories and show him a plain case of robbery with
violence, sad enough, but leaving no shameful shadow to darken
other lives.

Mrs. Hemmings was working at the table. She was humming tune-
lessly while she monotonously kneaded a golden mixture in a large
earthenware bowl. Taylor was seated near the range with her hands
in her lap.

"Good morning," said Guy quietly from the door. "I wonder if I
might have the loan of a chopper."

"Oh," exclaimed Mrs. Hemmings, putting her hand to her side,
"you gave me quite a turn! We're that on edge this morning. We
don't 'ave no choppers in 'ere. There should be one in the woodshed, round by the manure 'eap."

"Oh . . . er . . . thank you," said Guy.

"'Ave you discovered anythink yet?"

"We've made some progress."

"This place is like a death 'ouse," said Taylor. "They're not want-

100

ing lunch today, thank you. I rung the gong twice and then I went up to the old cat's bedroom and there they was, sitting round like a parcel of mutes—it was 'orrible."

"Death is horrible," said Guy. "I may as well tell you that we've found Miss Cathcart. Dead."

Mrs. Hemmings gave a stifled shriek. "There! I knew it. I said all along, as Taylor can bear me out, that she 'adn't gone off with no one." She sat down on a Windsor chair and her floury hands plucked at her apron. "Oh dear, oh dear! I do 'ate death in any form."

Taylor goggled at Guy. "What did she die of? She wasn't . . . done in, was she?"

"Yes," said Guy. "Hit over the head, perhaps with a chopper."

For a few moments, silence reigned in the kitchen. Guy was studying their reactions. Had they told him all that they knew? Aimlessly he wandered round the room, determined that they should speak first. Then he noticed something. The chopper was kept near the scene of the crime. Anyone might have picked it up. But if there was anything in his latest discovery he surely could rule out the tramp or murder for robbery.

At last Taylor broke the silence. "Thank Gawd, I've nothing to 'ide. I bet somebody will be all of a tremble when this gets into the papers."

Guy turned. "Who? This is a case of murder and it's your duty to tell the police all that you know."

"I didn't mean nothing. It was only a manner of speaking," stammered the parlormaid, startled by Guy's stern tone. "I never read of a murder without thinking 'ow 'orrible the one who's done it must be feeling."

"All right, all right! As long as you understand the position. If you notice anything the slightest bit strange or remember something you haven't told me, don't keep it under your hat. It's the little things that matter in my work. For instance, Mrs. Hemmings, where's your pound weight?"

Now it was Mrs. Hemmings' turn to be taken aback. "On the scales, I suppose. And if it isn't. . . ."

"I just noticed it wasn't."

"Then you'd better ask Ames. Borrows this and borrows that, without so much as a mention, to say nothing of thank you."

"But why should he borrow your weight?"

"For them pampered 'orses. I makes my pastry by guesswork, but that won't do for our four-footed friends."

"I thought you said she was 'it on the 'ead with a chopper," said Taylor, agog for the most gruesome details.

"Yes; that was my first idea; but, as I told you just now, it's the little things that matter when investigating a murder."

"Murder?" said a voice from the door, which was open, and there in the corridor stood Jessie, dressed in a blue and white cotton frock, blue shoes and a dark blue hat, tilted at the fashionable angle.

Mrs. Hemmings looked at Guy. He nodded. "Yes, Jessie, murder. We've found Miss Delia's body."

Jessie walked shakily into the room and crumpled into a chair. Guy watched her every movement. The corpse on the midden was clothed in pajamas and a woolen dressing gown. Delia couldn't have put her rawhide suitcase on the 11:35 slow: Jessie had gone into Melchester on the Saturday morning and Jessie had a blue outfit: Jessie was more upset than either Mrs. Hemmings or Taylor. Funge? Funge hadn't got much of a motive. It was motive that was holding him back.

While Guy was thinking, Jessie had begun to revive. "My legs are all of a tremble."

"You stay where you are for a while," said Mrs. Hemmings. "And we'll all 'ave a nice cuppa-tea."

"I can't. I've got to catch the two o'clock bus. I shall have to be getting along."

"Going to Melchester again?" asked Guy.

"Yes; heard of a place." She got slowly to her feet and steadied herself by the kitchen dresser. Then, anxiously, "'Ave you covered 'er up? I can't bear corpses."

"The ambulance has taken her away, but I'll walk with you as far as the gate if you don't like passing the midden," said Guy.

"The midden? Was that where you found her? Near the back gate into Lovers' Lane?"

"Yes. Does Funge smoke Woodbines?" asked Guy, keeping abreast with her train of thought.

Jessie may or may not have seen the import of his question, but she was beginning, he noted with regret, to get hold of herself. "Mr. Funge doesn't smoke much, and then it's something more classy than Woodbines; always something cork-tipped." Jessie led the way to the door and Guy followed.

Quite a lady she looks, Guy thought, on her afternoons out. I wonder if she'd open up, if I tried to get off with her. "You should always wear blue; it suits you, Jessie."

Brown eyes met blue. Starting to get fresh, was he? "I shall until winter. I likes little and nice, so one dress at a time is all that I 'ave."

"You're not like most girls. . . ."

"Being a detective makes you observant, don't it? Or is that what you always say?"

"I was only thinking a smart girl like you ought to come to London instead of being wasted down here."

Guy had piloted her down the drive to the left, tactfully avoiding the midden, and now they had reached the gate on the road.

"There's my bus waiting at the corner. So long, Mr. Northeast. We'll be seeing you, I expect."

Jessie ran down the road, leaving a thoughtful Guy to return to the house. The rock buns had been abandoned and Mrs. Hemmings and Taylor were eating chocolate cake and drinking tea. They offered him a cup of tea and a slice of cake, which he accepted gladly. Presently he asked, "Where's the housemaid?"

"She went back after dinner to finish in the bathroom. She's thorough, Elspeth is, but she's slow, and what with carrying up trays and waiting on the old lady, she's got be'ind."

"I want to speak to her," said Guy, setting down his cup. "I'll go up there."

There was a murmur of voices in Mrs. Cathcart's bedroom, but, walking quietly, he reached the bathroom unhindered. Elspeth took his news quietly. She agreed that it was a terrible thing and that the murderer must be brought to justice.

Guy explained that he had a few more routine questions to ask her. He believed it to be an outside job with robbery as the motive, but it was his duty to question everyone in the household, and he wasn't sure that Elspeth had been quite frank with him last time. Why had she denied that she was married?

Elspeth fell into the trap so helplessly that Guy felt mean. She said she didn't see what her state of life had to do with the murder of Miss Cathcart. Guy tried to explain that untruths or half-truths made people suspicious, and Elspeth, sitting on the edge of the bath, said that she hadn't seen her husband for years; that he was abroad—she thought in Australia. What was his name? His name, said Elspeth, was . . . er . . . Brent—Roger Brent; and, in answer to further questions, she had been married in a London registry office and she didn't know which, because it had been a runaway marriage and she had been all het up and she wasn't good at remembering names, anyhow. Guy put away his notebook with a sigh of exasperation.

"You're making things very difficult for me. Hadn't you better come clean?"

But that was no use. With a catch in her voice, Elspeth said that she had told him the truth and it wasn't her fault if she had a bad memory.

Guy became more and more suspicious. She was such a bad liar. This trail would have to be followed up and the marriage investigated. Probably there was nothing in it, but you never could tell. He couldn't eliminate Elspeth. Had she a blue dress? Well, she had and she hadn't; she'd got a patterned dress with quite a lot of blue in it. She'd show it to him if he liked. She'd nothing to hide. He waited on the back stairs and presently she came down with a limp and faded garment, which was blue enough and silky enough for a man, casting his mind back, to remember as the blue printed silk which had been suggested to him. Bother, thought Guy, and, with Elspeth's troubled gray eyes looking anxiously into his and her little gold head outlined by the sun that was pouring in through the backstairs window, was human enough to make one more appeal. "Now, my dear, why not tell me the truth?"

"I have," said Elspeth. "My husband's left me and I haven't done anything . . ."

Guy stamped downstairs. As he entered the kitchen, Mrs. Hemmings rose and shut the windows.

"Don't know who's listening," she explained in a mysterious whisper. "And I don't want to end up like Miss Delia. I asked Ames for my weight, sir, but 'e says 'e never 'ad it. And 'e seemed put out—said 'e'd got something else to do besides mucking about after my kitchen utensils."

"All right, Mrs. Hemmings. I'm going out to speak to him myself now."

In spite of all that Ames had to do besides mucking about after kitchen utensils, Guy found him standing at the orchard gate with his hands in his pockets, whistling through his teeth and staring at the blissful Flavia. When he saw Guy coming, he turned round and said, "Can I put the mare back in her box now? I don't want her down with the colic."

"Feed of grass won't hurt her. Do her good. You can take her in when I've had a talk with you."

"I've told you all I know."

"I wonder," said Guy, leading the way to the forage room. He sat down on the corn bin and slowly sharpened his pencil, leaving Ames to shift uneasily from one leg to the other. When his pencil had a nice sharp point and beads of sweat were showing on the groom's forehead, he said, "I suppose you've heard that Miss Cathcart's been found?"

"I've heard a lot of damn silly chatter down at the Dog and Duck."

"What were they saying?"

"That the old girl 'ad been biffed on the 'ead by a tramp."

Guy forced a laugh.

"It wasn't a tramp, I can promise you that. The body was found on your midden." His tone was accusing and Ames shuffled his feet again. "Very awkward for you, Ames. You're in charge of the midden and you've been extra lavish with straw the last few days."

"Natural, ain't it—without the old girl 'anging around?"

"Perhaps. Anyhow, I'm going to ask you a few questions. First, I ought to warn you that . . . ."

"Ask then, and cut out the funny stuff."

"All right, so long as we understand each other," said Guy, opening his notebook.

"Well, what is it you want?"

"I want a full account of your movements last Friday evening."

"I told you . . . ."

"You told me you spent the evening at the Dog and Duck and went home when they closed. Do you want me to put that down in my notebook?"

Ames hesitated.

"Supposing I didn't go straight 'ome, that doesn't mean I came back here."

"Of course it doesn't, but lies don't get us anywhere, Ames."

Ames continued to dither. His wife had the devil of a temper; God above knew what would happen if she found out where he'd been. Guy changed his tactics and gentled him, remembering that we've all something to hide, and at last he got a clear statement: Ames had left the Dog and Duck at approximately nine-thirty and had gone to visit a girl, Winnie Codstall was the name; she was general maid at Dunroamin, a bungalow on the Melchester road. Would the girl bear him out? She might and she mightn't and Ames didn't want to get her into trouble.

"Somebody's got a packet of trouble coming and we can't afford to be squeamish," replied Guy, noting the name of the house. Then suddenly he asked. "Where have you hidden the kitchen weight?"

"You mean the pound one. . . ?"

"Yes, I mean the pound one. Not the sort of thing you'd easily lose."

Slowly Ames remembered: it was back in the spring; Miss Delia had just bought the bay mare and he'd had orders that there was to be no more double handfuls, so he'd taken the trouble to find out exactly what quantities his measures held.

"And you've never had occasion to use it since?" asked Guy quietly.

"Never; and if those maids up at the 'ouse 'ave been telling you different I'll tell you for why. Spite, that's what it is, because I got on better with the old girl than what they did. You can't pin nothing on me for trying to keep a good place."

"Nobody's trying to pin anything on anybody, Ames. I'm trying to get at the truth. Then there's another matter—when did you last clean the house windows?"

Ames shot him a suspicious glance.

"Come on," said Guy, "I can find that out from others, you know."

"I only obliges. It's the gardener's job really, but 'e's getting on and don't fancy the ladder. There was nothing said about it the time I was engaged."

"You do clean them, then?"

"Once a fortnight—if they remembers."

"And did they remember . . . last Friday?"

"It wasn't Saturday, so it must of been Friday." Guy made a careful note in his book. "What's wrong with that?"

"Nothing, except it wasn't Saturday, Ames. What is your Saturday job?"

"Mucking round after the 'orses, the same as the rest of the week," said Ames, turning sulky again.

"You're never sent errands—into the village; or to Melchester, perhaps?"

"I wasn't hired to run errands."

"The horses keep you pretty busy, of course," said Guy soothingly. "Now, one last question—can you drive a car?"

"No."

"Got a license?"

"Only to drive a mo-bike, which I don't own, now that I'm married."

Guy pocketed his notebook.

"Let's 'ope you're satisfied now," said Ames, slouching off with a scowl on his face.

Glancing at his wristwatch, Guy walked down the drive to Lovers' Lane. The small police car was parked on the grass verge outside the gate; he hooted the horn and from the shrubbery appeared a red moon face framed in laurel leaves.

"Found anything more?"

"I've just 'appened on a dead cat, sir. 'E don't 'arf 'um. But we 'aven't come across anything resembling a lady's dress or 'andbag."

"I don't think you will on dry land. Concentrate on water, will you; anywhere between here and Melchester. And one of you keep an eye on the groom until you're relieved."

"Concentrate on water and keep an eye on the groom. Yessir."

Guy, who was no dashing motorist, turned carefully into the high road and drove at a steady thirty-five towards Melchester. He noticed the snug little bungalow, Dunroamin, but passed it; a man could be sent out from Melchester to check up Ames' statement; he himself had other fish to fry. He drove to the station and asked to see the ticket collector, Percy Janes. Janes, stocky, sensible and experienced, answered his questions with a directness which was refreshing after the evasions of Ames and Elspeth and the meanderings of the other maids. Janes wouldn't take it upon himself to swear that the lady, who had carried the rawhide suitcase, was dark, fair, young or old, though he might recognize her if he saw her again; he couldn't say definitely that her hat, handbag or shoes were blue. What he would swear to was that the general effect of her outfit was blue and that she was carrying a rawhide suitcase with black initials on it; he was positive of that because, as the lady had held out her ticket, she had let the suitcase swing round sideways and it had given him a biff on his shin. She hadn't apologized, but had walked straight through to the platform, and he hadn't looked after her; the knock had been nothing really, and there had been other passengers behind.

Guy had arranged to meet Dawes and the Chief Constable at five o'clock at the police station and this brief and businesslike interview left him with an hour to spare. He bought a bar of chocolate at the kiosk on the platform and walked out of the station munching thoughtfully. In the few hours which had passed since the discovery of the body he had got well away, but on paper the case looked as vague as ever, and he was going to be at a loss to find answers to such questions as, "What's your theory?" and, "Who's our man?" The long shot that he was going to try now would only add to the confusion, but he badly wanted to get all his suspects lined up, as it were, and take a good look at them. He turned his car and, absentmindedly crossing the High street with the traffic lights against him, drove past the police station and drew up in a quiet street, which led out of the market square.

Mr. Ross was in, and, on the strength of Guy's card, would see him in a very few moments. Mr. Forbes was out on his rounds, but would be back very soon. Guy sat in a waiting room with a large man and his small dog and a small woman and her large dog, and presently the voice of Mr. Ross could be heard assuring Lady Blakiston that the little fellow would be quite all right now, and a white-coated assistant put his head round the door and beckoned to Guy.

Mr. Ross was elderly and had the face of a retired naval officer, but his love of the horse was proclaimed by a yellow waistcoat, Derby-winner handkerchief and fox-mask tie. He had a man-to-man manner, offered a spot of whiskey, and was shocked to hear that a fine horsewoman like Miss Delia Cathcart had ended in such a sticky way. Forbes? Yes, Forbes had been out to Marley Grange lately, several times about the dog—overfeeding, of course—and twice, possibly three times, about the T.B. mare. No, Ross had received no complaint from Miss Cathcart and Forbes hadn't mentioned anything about a row. What sort of a fellow was Forbes? Oh, well . . . hum, ha. Forbes was a very able fellow, a brilliant fellow, only . . . Ross lifted his elbow and winked significantly.

Guy supposed that that explained why so able a man was working as an assistant, and Ross told him that at one time Forbes had had a very successful practice of his own. "Rotten piece of luck," he said charitably. "Killed a fellow while driving under the influence and they put him inside."

"Sad story. Is he a married man?"

"He's never mentioned a wife to me, but I believe there is one. Not living with him, of course. Look here, Inspector, I'm telling you all this because I know that, if I didn't, you'd find it out for yourself, but don't run away with the idea that David Forbes has anything to do with Miss Cathcart's death. Not that sort. When he's sober, he's as nice a fellow as you could find anywhere."

Guy reassured him. It had been mentioned that Forbes had reason to bear a grudge against Miss Cathcart, and, the case being cluttered up with suspects, he was anxious to eliminate him. He wanted a few words with him and, if he hadn't come back yet, would interview him at his private address later.

Ross supplied the address and advised Guy to call there early unless he wanted to spend the evening making a round of the pubs.

They shook hands and Guy, feeling not unlike an examination candidate, drove back through the center of the town to the police station.

As he had expected, it was, "Well, Northeast, what have you got for us?" and then it was, "But that gets us no forrarder," and, "Good God, man, can't you give us something definite?" Guy was tired and hungry; his shirt was sticking to him and life doesn't give you third chances; it would be the end of all his ambitions if he bungled this heaven-sent case. He said brazenly, "There's a lot behind all this. I want an opportunity to go over my notes and I can promise to let you have some definite conclusions in the morning."

Two unconvinced faces considered him. How *did* one dominate a situation? Probably by talking louder than anyone else. . . . He turned to the Superintendent and bawled out that he wanted a man sent at once to check Funge's alibi at his home and Ames' at Dunroamin. And the man was to report to Guy at his hotel that evening. Without fail. And another point: was there any news of Willoughby?

There wasn't? Right, Guy would see Mrs. Willoughby first thing in the morning. And what about the press? Was anybody dealing with them, because he'd like an appeal to Captain Willoughby to come forward. Good! He could leave that to Dawes. Then: had Dawes been to the bank? Good! Ten pounds, was it? Guy uttered a pregnant "Ha!" And had Dr. Baker reported the result of the P.M.? Not yet? Good heavens! It wasn't likely to help, but if the report came tonight it must be sent round to the Red Lion immediately; if not, Guy would pick it up first thing in the morning. Now he must be off. Good night, sir. Good night, Superintendent. He strode across the room, flung the door open and let it slam behind him.

The Chief Constable said, "By Jove, that feller's waking up a bit."

"Looks like it, said the Superintendent. "Good idea asking Willoughby to come forward. I had it in mind myself. . . ."

Meanwhile Guy, thankfully abandoning his new and exhausting personality, was strolling back to his hotel. He ate a substantial tea and then went out again to visit Forbes in his lodgings. Mr. Forbes wasn't back yet, said the slatternly landlady, but he was in by seven and the gentleman could wait in Mr. Forbes's sitting room, a lovely room on the first floor furnished with my'ogany and so clean that you could eat your dinner off the floor, but though you were on your 'ands and knees all day, there were some as were never satisfied. A trifle confused, Guy followed her up a stair that smelt of sour soup to a dark little room that overlooked a back yard, where grayish undergarments drooped from a sagging clothesline. "Lovely room," said the lady firmly, and left him.

Guy took a quick look round. There were whiskey bottles in the sideboard cupboard, a litter of unopened bills in the gimcrack writing desk. Mr. David Forbes used the aspidistra as an ashtray, sat with his feet on the mantelpiece and wasn't too hard-boiled to keep about him a few family photographs. The smiling lady with the locket and the Edwardian hairdressing was probably his mother; he had owned two adorable cockers and a nice stamp of lightweight hunter, and hullo, hullo . . . here, behind a cracked glass was a face Guy knew : the pale hair, the straight little nose, the steady, long-lashed eyes of Mrs. Cathcart's housemaid.

Or wasn't it? He took the photograph from its frame. "David from Elspeth. September, 1935."

Forbes very nearly caught Guy red-handed. The photograph was an excellent one and, where women were concerned, Guy was still a romantic. He stood gazing admiringly at the beautiful face and wondered how a man who'd had the luck to marry a girl like that could be so brutally careless of her happiness. A light step on the landing made him jump and brought him to his senses. He shoved the photograph back into its frame, replaced it on the mantelpiece and, by the time that Forbes was round the door, had his hands shoved in his pockets.

In spite of misfortune and, no doubt, incipient cirrhosis of the liver, David Forbes presented an extremely attractive appearance. He was tall and dark; he looked more like a Rupert than a David; the friendly grin with which he welcomed Guy was quite disarming. Guy explained himself. "Oh, good," said Forbes, offering cigarettes from a squashed packet. "I thought you were from some damned tradesman."

The relief in his charming voice sounded perfectly genuine, but Guy discounted it, summing him up as a gay deceiver. He said, "I'd like to know all you can tell me about the late Miss Cathcart."

Forbes had a poor opinion of the late Miss Cathcart. She was domineering, hard-boiled, had a face like a horse and a mind like a cesspool. The other Miss Cathcart—the one he'd seen about the overfed dog, the mousy one—was a complete nitwit, but the best of the family. The carroty one was as ugly as sin. . . .

Guy didn't want to know about the other Miss Cathcarts. There were some purely routine questions that he wanted to ask. It had come to his knowledge that the late Miss Cathcart had threatened to write to Mr. Ross about a mistake that had been made. . . .

Oh, that! Well, Forbes, with an engaging smile, couldn't deny that on the occasion of one of his visits to the Grange he'd had a couple and he'd made a slip of the tongue and ordered the wrong treatment. No earthly harm had been done, but, of course, the old bitch had gone off the deep end. . . .

All the same, Guy supposed, Forbes, with his unfortunate past, wouldn't want to lose his job? Oh, well, said Forbes, his face changing, at the present time there was a shortage of veterinary surgeons, but look here, what was Guy trying to pin on him? Once a man had been in trouble—even for something that might happen to anyone—it was always the same. If anything happened within a twenty-mile radius, the police were after him.

Guy denied that it was so. He'd had Forbes down on his list for questioning long before he'd heard of his—er—lapse. If Forbes could supply a satisfactory account of his movements on Friday night and Saturday morning, he'd hear no more about it.

Friday night? How the devil could a fellow remember what he'd done? He'd got back late from his rounds, that was certain, and then he'd have eaten one of Mrs. Willis's filthy meals and then he'd have gone out to some pub or other—damn it all, you couldn't expect a man to sit in this beastly little room twiddling his thumbs all evening. What pub? Probably he had started at the Crown and Anchor and gone on to the Red Lion and the Basket Makers' Arms. Someone might remember seeing him, but, as he never had any luck of any sort, it didn't seem likely. Oh, yes, he would have come back here when they closed, letting himself in with his latchkey.

Saturday morning? Yes, he remembered Saturday morning—always knocked off early on Saturdays and met a few chaps for a round. Last Saturday he'd had to go out to Little Hitherford to see a Clydesdale mare with grease and by the time he'd got back to Melchester *they* had opened. Yes, Guy was right; he'd have to pass the gates of Marley Grange on his way to Little Hitherford.

Guy's heart sank as he took down this inconclusive statement. Slow and rather solemn himself, he couldn't help admiring this graceful sinner, and he wasn't so successful that he couldn't sympathize with a hard luck story. He said, "That's the best you can do for yourself, is it?" and Forbes said it was, and Guy said, "Well, there's nothing makes me more suspicious than a really pat alibi." He shut his notebook and chattily remarked, "By the way, didn't I meet your wife this morning?"

Forbes' dark face hardened. He stuck his hands into his pockets, hunched his shoulders and said, "Damn clever fellow aren't you? I'm not married."

"Sure?"

"Unless I was drunk when I did it."

"Funny," said Guy, going over to the mantelpiece. "I could have sworn this was the photograph of someone I met this morning."

"A case of mistaken identity, Inspector. That's a girl I knew in the days of my innocent youth and she's living in Canada now. Who's her double? I shouldn't mind meeting her—was in love with the original once."

"Mrs. Cathcart's housemaid. Her Christian name's Elspeth. But you must have noticed the likeness. . . ?"

"Only been inside the house once; the door was opened by a snorty female who wasn't a bit like—er—Betty."

"Well, make a point of having a look at her next time."

"You bet I will, if there is a next time."

Refusing a whiskey and soda and an invitation to join Forbes at the Basket Makers' Arms later, Guy walked back to his hotel.

His room was high up, and the window looked across a narrow street to the blank wall of the Majestic cinema. It was open at the top, but there wasn't a breath of air in the room and bluebottles were buzzing angrily as they climbed the window panes. Guy pulled back the lace curtains and opened the window as wide as a broken sashcord would let him. The bluebottles flew out and more flew in. With a sigh he took a key from his pocket, unlocked the rickety wardrobe, pulled out a rawhide suitcase, dumped it on the whitish honeycomb counterpane, opened it and stood staring down at the selection of garments packed, or not packed, by Miss Delia Cathcart. The new climbing party of bluebottles buzzed angrily; taking the corner of the narrow street, a car mounted the pavement, bent a corporation lamppost and proceeded without reporting the accident; the sashcord gave up all together and with a malicious click the window closed itself, but Guy heard nothing. Since we've arranged our world like that, someone was going to hang for killing Delia Cathcart, and it was not through any flash of genius but through a slow man puzzling his head in a flyblown hotel bedroom, that the smug community would obtain its incongruous revenge. . . .

For some twenty minutes Guy stood staring down at the contents of the suitcase; then he reached for the old-fashioned pear-shaped switch above the bed and, after turning the light on by mistake, rang the bell. Coming along the corridor, he had passed a sensible-looking young chambermaid, but the girl who answered his summons was red-haired and rat-faced, with prominent teeth and bright, shifty eyes. However, she was a girl. . . .

He said, "I rang because I wondered if you could help me. I'm a police officer. . . ."

"Pardon?"

"I'm a police officer."

"Ooo! One of them there detecs?"

"That's right. You see, Miss . . . ?"

"Smallbone, my name is. And my Christian name's Sylvia."

"Well, Miss Smallbone, I've got a suitcase here. It's supposed to have been packed by a lady who was going away from home and may have been in rather a hurry. There's something about the things she packed that looks funny to me, but, being only a man, I don't understand the fashions and I want you to look at the things and tell me if there's anything about them that looks funny to you."

"I can do that for you," said the girl readily. "I likes to be up-to-date myself, and I've got good taste too. Lovely mauve jumper I bought yesterday. Five and eleven it was—none of your cheap muck for me. Only it don't mean that I shall get mixed up in anything, do it? I mean, I don't 'ave to go to court? Our Mum would go on awful if I got mixed up with the police."

Guy reassured her and, wiping her hands on her haunches, she advanced towards the bed.

"'Igh class underclothes," she giggled. "I like a bit more trimming myself. These plain silk things are chick, but they 'aven't got much sex appeal. That dressing gown must 'ave cost a lot, but it's dark for bedroom wear. I'd sooner 'ave a pastel shade edged with nostrich feathers, like you see on the films. These are good quality stockings. Evening dress." She shook out the brown lace dress and held it up against herself. "Too dark for my style, but quite distingy if she'd passed 'er first youth. Oh, 'ow 'ideous! Green satin sandals to wear with it . . . and then this dark red bag! Wot taste! You wouldn't catch me going out in all them different shades."

"They're not what the fashion papers call 'a contrast'?"

"That they're not. If she wanted a contrast to this brown dress, she'd 'ave 'ad gold or silver sandals and a gold or silver bag—never these green sandals. If she'd 'ad brown sandals, that matched 'er dress, then she might 'ave carried any colored bag. I dunno. . . ."

Miss Smallbone laid down the dress and placed the bag on it. "Well, she might 'ave chanced it, but it don't look nice."

Guy said, "It's all the more funny because there's a pair of brown sandals in her room at home. And several fancy bags. She wasn't— isn't a girl who has to make do, either. She's quite well off."

"I say," said Miss Smallbone in an awed whisper. "'As this got anything to do with the Marley vanishing case?"

"You've been such a help to me, Miss Smallbone, that I don't mind telling you it has. But you won't go talking about it, will you? I'm sure you can keep a secret. You look such a sensible girl."

"I've got my 'ead screwed on the right way," admitted Miss Small-bone. "And I'm not one to chatter. Now, if that two-faced Elsie 'ad been on duty . . . ."

"I was lucky," said Guy. "I rang the bell on the chance and then I found you. . . . Now, listen, Miss Smallbone: supposing a girl was in a hurry—would that account for her packing such a funny lot of things?"

"No, it wouldn't. 'Owever much of a nurry a girl was in it would be against her nature to take things that didn't *go*. I packed in a nurry once myself—I was in private service in London and a telegram come to say that our Mum was took bad—and, though I 'ardly knew what I was doing, when I got 'ome and come to unpack, except for forget-ting all my 'ankerchiffs, everything was OK. A girl might forget 'er 'ankerchiffs, or 'er 'ot water bottle, or 'er shoes, but what I mean is, either she'd pack the right-colored shoes, or not pack them at all."

"That's what I thought. Thank you very much, Miss Smallbone. You've been a great help."

"Don't mention it. And you needn't fear that I'll go round chat-tering. It'll be a secret," said Miss Smallbone, looking up at him, "between you and me."

"That's right," said Guy, folding up the dress and replacing it in the suitcase. "Well, thanks awfully . . . ."

But beyond taking up a more permanent position with her back against the bedrail, Miss Smallbone made no move.

"Fancy you being one of them detecs," she mused. "Dangerous job, ain't it? But I should think you're brave."

"Oh, there's not much danger about it," said Guy, shutting up the suitcase. "It's generally rather dull."

"Ever copped a murderer?"

"No," said Guy firmly. He looked at his wristwatch and put a mundane question. "Do you think the bathwater's likely to be hot now?"

"Well, it's never what you might call 'ot, but you can get a nice bath if you're the first. I'll go unlock the door and turn the water on."

Guy heaved a sigh of relief as the door closed behind her. He got out of his sticky clothes and avoided Miss Smallbone's ambush by lurking in a dark corner till a bell summoned her to the other end of the corridor.

The tepid bathwater brought no fresh inspiration, but it was refreshing, and, back in his bedroom, he felt competent and cool. He collected his fountain pen and a writing block, sat down in the armchair by the window and set to work on the job—never congenial to him—of turning his thoughts into words.

He began by writing in block capitals the words OPPORTUNITY and MOTIVE. No sooner were they written than there was a knock at the door. If it's that girl, I'll wring her neck, said Guy to himself, but it wasn't Miss Smallbone: it was the moon-faced constable, who, before leaving the Grange, had received orders by telephone from the Superintendent to check the alibis of Funge and Ames. Guy, already put out by the interruption, was annoyed to find that the Superintendent had entrusted enquiries, which needed tact, to this bumpkin, but the man seemed to have done the job competently: Mrs. Funge, well-spoken of in the village, testified to having heard her son enter the cottage as the lovely clock in her front room struck eleven; Miss Winnie Codstall would admit nothing and deny nothing and wasn't to be trusted whatever she said.

Guy dismissed the constable and turned back to his writing block. OPPORTUNITY and MOTIVE. What the devil had he meant by writing that down? Slowly he forced his mind back into the interrupted train of thought, and now in column form beside the first two words, he added the names of his suspects: Ames; Funge; Forbes; Willoughby. A few moments' thought convinced him that opportunity would have to be viewed from more than one angle: first, the opportunity of committing the murder between eleven p.m. on the Friday night and dawn on the Saturday morning. Mightn't he narrow this down a little? Miss Cathcart hadn't been killed in her bed; according to the Superintendent's report, there had been no blood on the blankets. It was highly probable, therefore, that she had been aroused by the whistle which Mrs. Hemmings had heard. Was it a prearranged signal? (If so, Ames or Willoughby were the most likely callers.) Or was it intended for one of the maids? (If so, Funge or Forbes were the most likely callers, and the crime might have been caused by Delia getting up to poke her nose into other people's business.) But whoa, Guy told himself; keep to facts, man! Who had weak or no alibis for the hours of darkness? Ames, since the girl at Dunroamin hadn't backed up his story; Willoughby, who had got home late from a bridge party and had left home at dawn. Forbes had put up an impractical alibi. Funge? Guy gathered his mother was a reliable witness.

He was warming to his work. Under OPPORTUNITY he would give each of his suspects marks: Ames, Willoughby and Forbes five out of five; and Funge, perhaps, two.

And now for another angle—the suitcase. The murderer had certainly placed this on the train to suggest that Delia had traveled to London. The packing of the bag implied access to Delia's bedroom. Ames had cleaned the windows on Friday: again, five, no, four marks, to him. Funge had no reason to enter the house, but possessed a likely accomplice in Jessie: five marks to him. Forbes, with Elspeth as his accomplice, had equal opportunity with Funge, so five marks to him. Willoughby? Delia might have packed it herself and brought it out to the garden, but, then, where was her dress? No, he couldn't accept the Dawes' theory. Mrs. Willoughby had been alone in Delia's bedroom on the Friday, but then you were dealing with a premeditated crime and Mrs. Willoughby was an accessory before the act. He couldn't give more than two marks for that.

That didn't finish the suitcase. The murderer must have had the opportunity to plant the suitcase in the train. Funge and Jessie had gone into Melchester by car on the Saturday morning. They scored the maximum for that. Willoughby had left his car at the Station Garage: five marks also to him. Forbes had admitted passing the gates of Marley Grange and returning to Melchester round about eleven: five marks to him. Ames said that he had never left the Grange that morning and there was no evidence that he had. (He must check up on that.) Two marks? No, one mustn't be prejudiced. One mark to Ames.

Now, MOTIVE. What could have impelled anyone to kill this woman? Take Ames first again—was it the old story of Potiphar's wife and Joseph? Was Ames just an animal, intent on satisfying his brutish instincts? Had Delia, the sex-starved spinster, led him on only to refuse at the last fence, or had her importunities exasperated him into silencing her forever? A fine choice of unsavory stories, so five, no, four marks to Ames. Then Willoughby, a man of Delia's own class with a tiresome wife: half the tragedies in the world were based on that eternal triangle. Definitely, five marks to Willoughby. Now

Forbes and Funge. Delia had threatened both, but to what did her threats amount? Possibly the loss of their jobs, but more probably just a reprimand from their employers, and we don't risk swinging for that. One mark only to each of them.

And now he could apply his recent deductions. The murderer (or his accomplice) had packed the bag with garments that didn't match: what was the probability of each of his suspects making such a mistake? Ames, hurried, ignorant and a man, must score five marks. Elspeth, working for Forbes, refined and with taste as good or better than Delia's, was most unlikely to have erred; and Forbes scored nothing. Jessie was a rougher type than Elspeth . . . well, one mark to Funge. Mrs. Willoughby? She dressed sloppily but to the character that she invented for herself, and that argued clothes sense. Nought for the gallant Captain.

And now, before he added up, he might give marks for his own impressions. Funge, a quarrelsome Bolshy fellow, whose bark was worse than his bite, who hadn't really much guts, should have two marks out of five. Forbes, pleasant when sober, but no doubt inclined to be quarrelsome in his cups, three marks. Ames, a low type, sullen, a liar, five out of five: he could give rein to his prejudices this time. Willoughby was an unknown quantity still, and for that the symbol was X.

X? What price another unknown quantity . . . somebody who hadn't appeared on the stage yet, somebody whose opportunities hadn't been enquired into, whose movements hadn't been investigated; in short, the murderer? Mr. X would get full marks *every* time.

His chart was completed. He added up the marks and surveyed the totals.

Suspects	Opportunity			Motive	Mistake	Type	Total
	Murder	Packing	Planting				
Ames	5	4	1	4	5	5	24
Funge	2	5	5	1	1	2	16
Forbes	5	5	5	1	0	3	19
Willo'by	5	2	5	5	0	x	17?
"X"	5	5	5	5	5	5	30

There was no doubt about it. The Chief Constable and Dawes, pushing along like senseless battering rams, would press for an early arrest and Ames would be their man. But no jury would convict. With a sigh Guy realized that tomorrow would have to be given over to work on a case against Ames, but he determined that no amount of "What have you got?" and "Give us something definite" would drive out of his mind the last man on his list, the one who had scored full marks on every court . . . Mr. X.

He put his writing materials away and got wearily into bed. It was time to call Thursday a day. The management of the Red Lion ignored such luxuries as bedside lamps, so he was unable to distract his mind by reading, and the burden of his thoughts was MOTIVE. If only he had met Delia, he might have been able to say why she was killed. He was working in the dark. If only he knew the motive. . .

Sleep when it came was disturbed by dreams. "Come along now, Northeast," said the Chief Constable, turkey-red. "Come along, come along Northeast," said the Superintendent, thrusting out his jaw. Guy tried to answer, opened his mouth, but no words came. "Come along, Northeast," they said in swelling chorus. "Come along, come along."

FRIDAY

GUY WAS UP early next morning. He had sent out for the newspapers, and, down in the coffee room, neglecting a desiccated grapefruit and a cup of grayish coffee, he unfolded them. Under such headlines as "Hatchet Fells Horsewoman" and "Dreadful Discovery on Dung Heap," the London papers, with airy inaccuracy, emphasized the human side of the story. Delia was a leader of county society; Delia was the chatelaine of a magnificent mansion standing in its own grounds: Delia was a fresh-faced girl little dreaming of the fate in store for her; Delia was in turn musical, a well-known figure in the hunting field, the Lady Bountiful of Marley village, an elderly woman of retiring disposition seldom seen outside the old-world cottage that had been in possession of the Cathcart family for three, four, five hundred years. Delia had slept in the garden, strolled in the garden; her skull had been cracked, split, battered by a blunt hatchet, a sharp hatchet, a hammer; she had had many men friends; she had had no men friends; the murderer had left no clue to his identity; the police were in possession of several valuable clues. In spite of these differences of opinion, each account carried in its tail the same sting: in the case of the Marley murder there would be none of the usual bungling since Scotland Yard had immediately been called in.

Guy turned to the local paper. The *Melchester Mercury's* account was strictly accurate and extremely dull, but the sting was there all right. No sooner was Miss Cathcart's disappearance reported by her family than, with his usual acumen, the well-known and highly efficient Superintendent Dawes was on the scene. The powers that were, however, had thought fit to take matters out of his capable hands, and the supermen from Scotland Yard were now in charge. The

119

Melchester Mercury was therefore confident in predicting that an early arrest would be made. On the picture page was a photograph of Dawes looking noble, and one of Guy, taken at the time when he was bungling the case of Lady Oughborough's emeralds, looking like a boiled owl.

Guy laid aside the papers and started on his skinny grapefruit. He was up against it now, he thought grimly; if he mucked up this case he'd not only let himself down, but the Yard. And the Yard wasn't fond of its failures; the man who blundered was responsible for his blunder; there were no benevolent departmental petticoats under which you might hide. Probably at this moment in his flat at Putney, Superintendent Hannay was reading his newspaper and wondering what sort of a fool Northeast would make of himself this time; soon, on his way to the Yard, he would be thinking the case over, wondering whether, since this was homicide and it's homicide that gets the publicity, it would be wise to recall Northeast from Marley and send down a more capable man. Guy could see the lids droop over Hannay's gray eyes as he pondered. He wasn't a man who suffered fools gladly; he wouldn't think, give the fellow a chance, or, poor devil, this will make or break him: he'd think only of the prestige of the Yard.

Guy pushed away the remains of the grapefruit, and, getting coffee and bacon and eggs down into his empty stomach, thought, it's a long lane that has no turning, and, one swallow doesn't make a summer, and, it's always darkest before dawn. After all, there wasn't anything abnormal about him; he was no Adonis and no genius, but his mental and physical equipment was as good as the next man's. No one went through life without making mistakes; you were young; you'd been lucky, and you were much too sure. But you learned from your mistakes; you learned that the way to get up a hill is not to keep your eyes fixed emulously on the summit, but to watch your feet going down one after the other till you found that there was level ground beneath them, and looked up, and saw that you were there. Then everybody who didn't know the trick praised you. Marvelous, they said, and asked you how it was done, but if you told them, they wouldn't believe you. Success in life couldn't be due to a prosaic faculty for keeping on keeping on: they wanted to excuse themselves, saying, it's not my fault that I've no talents. . . .

In a considerably heartened mood, Guy walked round to the police station. The Chief Constable was already there. He smelled of soap and his red face glowed with early morning freshness.

"Good morning, Inspector," snapped Dawes, exhaling germicide, and the Chief Constable heartily shouted, "Well, Northeast, how are you this morning? Ready to make an arrest?"

Guy's bolstered-up spirits sank abruptly. He said, "I don't know about that, sir. It doesn't do to get the wrong man—or the right one on insufficient evidence."

"Seen the newspapers? They seem to expect something spectacular. World's got its eye on you, Northeast."

Dawes cut the cackle. "Perhaps the Inspector will let us know the result of his last night's deliberations."

Not without satisfaction Guy laid his neat chart on the table. He hadn't expected that it would be particularly well received by Dawes, but he had felt sure that the Chief Constable, as a military man, would approve of it. But Major Carruthers had never worn a brass hat. "What's this? What's this?" he shouted irritably.

Guy explained the chart and, step by step, his reasoning. "Oh well," said the Chief Constable, setting his brain to work with the air of a man who winds up a magnificent machine for a probably futile purpose, "let's get down to it. Take this column One. Now, Northeast, how many men really have alibis for the hours they spend in bed, and that's when the crime was committed? What I mean is, a married man can say he was in bed with his wife, but she isn't evidence. A single man may go to bed all right and then pop through the window."

"Exactly," said Dawes. "In this case, to consider opportunity gets us absolutely nowhere."

"I agree," said the Chief Constable, "and then this column headed Motive. I knew Delia Cathcart well, and I can't imagine anyone having any reason for murdering her. And there's one idea you've got in your head, Northeast, which I'm still convinced is sheer nonsense. She wasn't the sort of young woman to muck around with a groom."

Guy was ready with an answer, but Dawes interrupted him. "This man, Forbes, sir. He's our man. Just the type. All right sober, but violent when drunk and doesn't know what he's doing."

Guy began, "I thought Ames was your fancy," but he was shouted down again, this time by the Chief Constable.

"Look here, the time's come for action, not for talk. Northeast—what's your program for this morning?"

Guy sat for a moment looking down on his discredited chart. Oh fools and blind, he thought, the light growing. And since they were the fools, he could suffer them. "You're right, sir," he said. "It's no use concentrating on the vague time we have for the murder. We have one fixed time element—the time that the woman in blue passed the barrier at the station. I'm going to pin everyone down to their movements that morning. Only the murderer can have planted the suitcase. . . ."

"A woman?" said Dawes. "I shouldn't have thought it was a woman's crime."

"I was going on to say, sir, that if the murderer was a man, he must have had a female accomplice. . . ."

"Oh, good God, another needle in the haystack! What you'd better do, is to get going, Northeast."

Guy rose to his feet. "Very well, sir."

"Just a minute," said Dawes. "I've got the report of the P.M. here—nothing to add to what Doctor Baker told us. And there's one piece of information—definite information—that I collected yesterday. The cashier from the bank came in to tell me that the notes he gave Miss Cathcart were new ones and he happens to have a note of their numbers."

Guy gave Dawes a bit of his own back. "That's not much help, if the handbag's at the bottom of a horse pond." But a second thought was better and he was honest enough to speak it. "But, of course, the murderer may have taken the notes out. Very few of us would be strong-minded enough to throw ten pounds away. We may get some useful news if you advertise the numbers."

His honesty did him no good. When he had gone the Chief Constable said, "My God, how that fellow does shilly-shally."

"I don't like to run a man down, sir," said the Superintendent, "but I'm afraid he's proving a washout. That chart now—did you notice he'd put 'X' at the bottom, and given him full marks? Childish, I call it, when 'X' is an imaginary person. . . ."

Guy walked round to the garage. His ears weren't burning, but he felt sure that the two men he had left were talking him over. Well, they had asked him what his program was and he had begun to tell them, but they'd been too impatient to listen; get going! they'd shouted before he'd had time to remind them that it's because of their mistakes that murderers swing, and to tell them that it was not by shouting out, "Here's our man!" and hounding first one and then another of their suspects, but by concentrating on a trivial discrepancy that he would solve this puzzling case. On the whole he was glad that they hadn't listened to him; they had no use for theories; he could see now that the best way to handle them was to keep them in the dark until his evidence was complete.

He drove through the center of the town and drew up in a side street beside a window crowded with unappetizing but highly colored cakes. At this early hour the staff of the Cosy Cafe were not prepared for customers and as he entered the shrill squeals of a feminine quarrel met his ears. "Somebody's lying!" "Well, it's not me. I'm a respectable girl, I am." "Oh, go and roll!" Guy coughed, and with a triumphant toss of her head a platinum blonde waitress stepped through a curtain of bamboo and beads.

It wasn't the platinum blonde who had served coffee and cakes to a chauffeur and a dark girl probably dressed in blue last Saturday morning; if it had been, she would have remembered for she was a noticing sort and took a real interest in the customers. She was ever so sorry not to be able to help. What was the trouble? Oh, the chauffeur had had money left him, had he? Lucky chap! There were ever so many things she wanted, but money didn't come her way. Yes, of course Guy could see the other young lady, but it was doubtful if she'd be able to tell him anything. Some people didn't use their eyes.

The blonde screeched, "Doris!" and a more homely girl came through the beads. With a meaning look at her colleague, she did remember serving a chauffeur and his young lady; she remembered it because she had never seen a girl eat so many cream buns. Yes, she could tell Guy the time to a minute because the Minster clock had been striking eleven as the couple came in, and it had struck half past before they had left—she knew that because, as the chauffeur had sat down, he had said, "What a din," only he had used a nasty word, and when the half hour struck she had been adding up his bill and he had asked her if the noise didn't get on her nerves, and she had said that it used to, but it didn't now. No, he hadn't hurried off. He had waited outside the shop for his young lady, who had gone to the . . . er . . . cloakroom.

With rising spirits Guy drove out to Marley and down the lane which led to the Willoughby's farm. Halfway down the lane he saw Mrs. Willoughby in a green smock and broad-brimmed hat, sitting on a camp stool and sketching a view of distant fields. "You may call me an escapist," she said. "Certainly I have only to take up my pencil to find myself in another world."

"I hate to bring you back," Guy said, "but there's a question I want to ask you and then I hope not to have to worry you again. Where were you last Saturday morning between eleven and twelve?"

"My dear man, how do I know? I'm too intelligent to worry about something that isn't. Time isn't. It only exists for the benefit of the insane majority. . . ."

"I know," said Guy, "but I'm one of them and I'm asking you this question because I'm investigating a case of murder. Please try to cast your mind back. . . ."

"Why should I? A horse-faced woman has died, but what's death?"

"I see your point of view," said Guy, wondering what the Chief Constable and Dawes would make of this aggravating woman. "But seriously, Mrs. Willoughby, if you answer my question now, you won't have any more trouble. If you don't, you'll have endless policemen coming out here to ask you endless questions, and they're sure to come just when you're in the mood for sketching."

Gerda Willoughby winced at the word "sketching," but the point went home. She said, " Oh, all right, but it's the end of my morning's work. Saturday was the day my husband went off, wasn't it? Well, I hung about here thinking how sordid it all was, and later, when the car had come back, I went into Melchester."

"And what did you do there?"

"I bought things. I remember a pyramid of oranges—all the brightness and sweetness of Old Spain."

"A fruit shop?"

"A stall in the market place. I hate smug shops."

"What time were you there?"

"Eleven o'clock. I heard the Minster tell the hour—lovely strong bells used for an ignoble purpose. . . ."

"And then?"

"Oh, then I went to Woolworth's and bought some clothes pegs and a sink strainer. There were lots of other things on my list, but I forgot to look at it till I was half way home."

"A stall at the market and then Woolworth's. I'm afraid there's not much chance of anyone remembering you."

"Why should they?" asked Gerda Willoughby, goggling her pansy velvet eyes at him. "If you're trying to establish alibis, or whatever you call them, why do you pick on that time—eleven to twelve? I don't often read the newspapers—so sordid—but this morning I did happen to glance at a picture paper, which I take for the maids. It said that Delia Cathcart was found dead in her dressing gown, and, from what I know of her, I'm sure she wouldn't have been in her dressing gown after half past eight or nine."

Guy thought he would go mad if he talked any longer to Gerda

Willoughby, so, after giving her a chance to produce a firmer alibi and getting a dissertation on the nonexistence of place, he tore himself away and drove to the Dog and Duck, where he ordered his usual lunch of bread and cheese and bitter. It was only by chance that, as he leaned against the bar waiting for someone to attend to him, he saw printed in block capitals on a cardboard sheet propped on the mantelpiece, the name, Ames. Idle curiosity, or the habit of casting his net wide, took him across the room. S. Ames, he learned, had reached the final of the Marley Green Darts Competition.

"I see you're having a darts competition," he said, when Mr. Hogmore had wished him good morning and expressed satisfaction at seeing him back again, and Hogmore said, yes, it was an annual event and there were several first-rate players in the village. "The final's on tonight," said Hogmore. "'Arris v. Ames. Worth seeing that'll be, if you 'appen to 'ave 'arf-a-nour to spare."

Guy said he'd have to be back in Melchester and went on to ask which of the two men was likely to win. Harris, it appeared, was steady, but Ames, though erratic at times, was brilliant when his back was against the wall. It had been a treat to see him last Saturday morning; he'd started like one of the Sunday evening motoring crowd, but at the end he'd been playing like a bloody automaton.

"Saturday morning? But how did they manage to play it then? Isn't this the fellow who was groom to the late Miss Cathcart?"

"That's right. Well, you see, it was like this. What with the chaps working late haymaking and young Fred 'Arris being laid up with a poisoned finger, we'd got be'ind, and, so, Miss Cathcart not being about, Ames slips out and we sends word to Fred, who couldn't get off in the afternoon or evening, being footman at the 'All. That," said Mr. Hogmore placidly, "was 'ow it was arranged."

Guy suggested, "Awkward for Ames if he'd been caught. By all accounts Miss Cathcart wouldn't have stood for that kind of thing."

"Ah well, it was just on eleven when Stanley come in 'ere and Miss Cathcart, she'd properly vanished by then. Them other two—Miss Sheila and Miss Nancy—they don't take much notice. Soft, they are."

"Sporting of him to risk it, though. He must have been away . . . well, for how long?"

"What with talking it over friendly and drinks all round, 'e was gone about a nour. But there, nothing venture, nothing win, specially when you're young. Now what'll you 'ave, sir? We've got a tasty bit of cheddar in today. . . ."

Guy ate his lunch outside in the sunshine and his despised and neglected chart was spread on his knee. Ames, because he was a man, might well have made a mistake in packing a woman's evening outfit; he'd scored full marks in the column headed Mistake, but now a thick black line went through his name. Blasted idiot! To cover a small fault, which was none of Guy's business, he'd lied, concealing the very fact which would have taken him off the list of suspects yesterday. And Funge and Jessie were off, and that left Forbes and Willoughby, and in the "Mistake" column neither Forbes nor Willoughby had scored any marks at all. Now that Ames was off, only X had full marks in that column. Then, X, why did you err?

Guy ate his lunch as quickly as anyone can eat bread and cheese, and, since escaping from Mr. Hogmore was child's play to a man accustomed to escaping from Gerda Willoughby, he was soon on his way to Marley Grange. Elspeth opened the door and before she could usher him into the inner hall he said, "I had a nice talk with your husband yesterday."

It was a slight variation from the old, "All is discovered—fly," but Elspeth was deceived. She said, "So he told you . . . ?"

Guy didn't answer that, but asked, "What was the point of concealing it?"

"No one knew about it," explained Elspeth. "I came here when he was in prison—I had to do something. When he came out, I wouldn't go back to him. I know it sounds awful, but it wasn't only the drink; there were other women. Then he took this job with Mr. Ross, and he found out where I was, and he comes to see me sometimes—mostly when he's short of money."

"When did you see him last?"

"Last Saturday morning. He wanted money. I told him Miss Delia was missing and he made rather a fuss."

"Yes?" said Guy encouragingly.

"I don't want to get him into trouble."

"He has only himself to blame for any trouble that's coming." Guy's voice had become very grim. "Did he threaten you?"

"Not exactly. He said I wasn't to tell anybody I knew him and that he didn't want anybody to know we were married."

"Ye-es. Did he say why?"

"I don't think he did; but I gathered he'd had a row with Miss Delia over one of the horses. And he said, I remember now, that 'he'd opened his mouth in a pub.' Of course," said Elspeth anxiously, "that might happen to anyone. I mean what a man says when he's drunk doesn't mean anything."

"Possibly not, but you'd have saved me a lot of trouble if you'd told me all this to begin with. The police generally find out things in the end. Now would you ask if I can see Mrs. Cathcart?"

"She's in bed. It's her heart and the doctor comes every day."

"Anyhow, tell 'them' I'm here."

Elspeth went to find out if 'they' would see him and he had time for thought. He mustn't be bamboozled by a beautiful face. Had Elspeth gone into Melchester with Forbes? There and back, if you rushed, wouldn't take more than half an hour in a car. Had Elspeth planted the suitcase? Or was Forbes' accomplice one of his other women? Then Dawes could *cherchez*. Dawes could get busy in Melchester and *cherchez la femme*.

Elspeth returned to say, "Miss Cathcart will see you." Sheila and Nancy were sitting in the drawing room. Sheila, sprawled in an armchair, was doing nothing, but Nancy, surrounded by skeins of colored wool, was intent on a square of *petit point* needlework. Both wore simple black dresses.

Guy shirked the few words of sympathy he had strung together in the drive. He said, "I wanted to make sure it was all right about the inquest tomorrow."

"Oh," said Sheila. "You understand it's quite impossible for Mother to attend. She's not got over the shock and the doctor has forbidden it. We haven't quite decided yet which of us is coming."

"Darling," said Nancy, "we decided at breakfast that I'd better go."

Guy intervened, "I rather think the Chief Constable is expecting you both."

"I know; that's what the Chief Constable said, but we can't both leave Mother. And after all, I am the eldest, Nancy."

"But, darling," replied Nancy, "you're so much better with Mother." She turned pathetic eyes to Guy. " I can't bear seeing people suffer."

"The police are so inconsiderate," said Sheila. "And it isn't as though this wasn't a house of mourning. Is it really necessary for Jessie and Elspeth to attend? Maids are such dreadful ghouls. We don't want them talking over our darling, do we, Nancy, dear?"

An idea which had been at the back of Guy's mind suddenly took shape. "I came to tell you that we shall want not only Jessie and Elspeth, but Mrs. Hemmings and Taylor too. You see we never know who the coroner will decide to ask for."

"Then that settles it, darling," said Sheila blankly. "It will have to be the big car."

"But if we both go, who will look after poor Mother?"

Guy suggested, "Mightn't the district nurse look in for an hour or two?"

"The district nurse?" exclaimed Sheila in horror. "She's maintained by subscriptions. Mother wouldn't like that."

"Why can't our darling be laid away quietly," said Nancy piteously, "without all these dreadful arrangements?"

Guy made sympathetic noises and waited for them to settle something. At last Sheila made up her mind. "It will have to be Nurse Radcliffe. It isn't as if Mother disliked her and, after all, she was a V.A.D. in the war."

"I suppose," said Nancy, "it is the only possible arrangement. I do hope the coroner will understand and not keep us hanging about."

"I rather gather," said Guy, "that the proceedings tomorrow will be purely formal. I see no reason why you shouldn't be back here in nice time for lunch."

Sheila groaned and Nancy shuddered at the mere thought of food on the day of the inquest, so Guy quickly changed the subject by putting "one last little routine enquiry."

"It's not really important, of course, but we like to have everything tidy and there appears to be a small hiatus in my notes as to the servants' movements last Saturday morning, the day the disappearance was discovered. Jessie, now . . . ?"

"Jessie went into Melchester without permission," said Nancy quickly. "Don't you remember how annoyed Mother was, darling?" Sheila remembered now that it was mentioned and Guy made an elaborate note, before asking, "And the others?"

Sheila remembered distinctly seeing Mrs. Hemmings and Taylor and Nancy wasn't sure that she had noticed Elspeth. "Might she have slipped out without either of us noticing, darling?" Sheila cast her mind back. "It was Saturday—her day for doing the housemaid's cupboard . . . I can distinctly hear Mother saying, 'You can leave it till later, Elspeth.'"

"Yes, darling. When we went upstairs with the Superintendent . . . ?"

"Ye-es. "

"What time would that be?" asked Guy.

"It must have been just about twelve," said Nancy. "A little before, I should think."

"No, Nancy, a little after, because—don't you remember, darling?—we had early lunch as soon as the Superintendent had left."

"You can't fix the time closer than that?" asked Guy, not quite satisfied.

Sheila wrinkled her brows, then asked Nancy, "What time was it when you got back from your runaround in the car?"

"I don't remember, darling. We were all so fussed that time didn't seem to matter. I know the Superintendent was here."

"Ah, then I'll ask him," said Guy shutting his notebook. "It's of no great importance."

Guy could never leave gracefully. Now the only farewell he could think of was, "Well, *au revoir* till the inquest," and that wouldn't quite do. Instead, he took an interest in Nancy's embroidery. "That's very pretty, but isn't it rather trying for the eyes?"

Nancy explained that she could sew all day and her eyes never ached, and Sheila volunteered that her eyes started to water if she even attempted to sew on a button. Guy then remembered his head had ached rather a lot lately and Sheila told him he couldn't go to a better oculist than Mr. Walton, 16, Giles' Square; they all, even Nancy, went to him once a year, just to see that nothing was wrong. Guy gratefully wrote down the name and address, complimented Nancy again on her work, and, at last, got out of the room.

In the drive, by his car, the moon-faced constable was waiting.

"Found 'em, sir," he said in a hoarse whisper.

"What—the whole lot?"

"Yessir. Dress, shoes, 'andbag and 'at, wrapped up in brown paper. In a pond, as you said, just off the road, not 'alf a mile from the 'ouse. The brown paper parcel also contained a pound weight, seemingly off some kitchen scales. Not knowing has you were 'ere, I despatched Chart with them to the station, while I remained in observation 'ere, sir."

"Good," said Guy and drove quickly back to Melchester singing hymns. It was beginning to open and shut. A few more enquiries and he'd have a case for a jury. He'd been lucky that morning, but he was on to it anyhow and if you stuck to your job you deserved any luck that was going. With the inquest at twelve tomorrow, he had a busy evening before him. A chat with the ticket collector first at the station; then he ought to call and see—no, he'd look such a fool if he was wrong! He'd better verify his idea by reference to an encyclopedia; there must be a public library in Melchester. He must get his case perfect before he opened up to the Chief Constable or Dawes. Then he'd have to pretend to be modest.

Here were the streets of Melchester. Guy had hoped that it wouldn't be necessary for him to see Dawes again that day, but Dawes was seated at his desk; the damp objects, which had been Delia Cathcart's London clothes, were spread before him and with piercing but unseeing eyes he was looking them through and through.

Guy said, "No fingerprints, of course, sir?"

"No."

"Any notes in the bag?"

"No money at all. The contents of the bag are: Three handkerchiefs; a letter signed G. Marchmont, asking if a certain horse, presumably offered for sale by Miss Cathcart, has ever been known to buck, rear, bolt, pull, crib-bite, wind-suck or . . . er . . . bore. A powder compact with a horse's head on it. A button. Two hairpins. A receipted bill from the local saddler. A safety pin. A snapshot of a span'el. A cookery recipe cut out from a newspaper. Two cigarette cards. And a piece of string."

"In fact the normal contents of a lady's handbag—except for the absence of cigarettes, half a dozen boxes of matches, two or three lipsticks and a pot of paste rouge. Now, we want to trace a few of the notes."

"Yes, the case is breaking nicely," said Dawes.

"I've been doing a round of the pubs. Funny how some fellows start talking when they've had one or two. Listen to this, Northeast." Superintendent Dawes thumbed over his notebook. "'She's an interfering old bitch and, by God, I'm not going to stand any nonsense. I don't like hitting a woman, but D.C.'s a sour-winded old mare.' "

"That's threatening language, right enough."

"Yes; and said before those who are ready to swear to it. We'll soon be getting our man."

Guy couldn't resist saying, "By 'our man,' you mean Forbes, I take it, not Ames?"

"Of course I mean Forbes. I admit I did suspect the groom at one time, but I believe in keeping an open mind."

"Yes, I've noticed that, sir," said Guy and met the Superintendent's keen look with blank blue eyes. However, the Superintendent hadn't passed thirty years in the force without learning how to keep inspectors in their place.

"What you've got to do now, Northeast, is to concentrate on our case against Forbes. I think we can consider Ames, Funge and Willoughby definitely out. What I can't quite see yet is how Forbes got that suitcase planted."

"His wife told me . . . ."

"His wife, did you say? That's a new one on me."

Guy thought it best to apologize handsomely. "I ought to have mentioned it before. His wife is Elspeth, the housemaid at the Grange."

"When did you discover that?"

"I got a line on it yesterday, but I only got it really established this afternoon. As I was saying, Mrs. Forbes told me that there were other women. So I was wondering whether we had not better get on a line on his Melchester lady friends. He may have used one of them to plant the suitcase."

"Why not the wife?"

"She's more or less got an alibi; at least it depends what time you were at the Grange on Saturday morning. Did you happen, sir, to make a note of the time?"

Dawes referred to his notebook. "11:10 a.m., Saturday, July 2nd, took call from Marley Grange, reporting Miss Delia Cathcart missing; proceeded to Marley by car; arrived Marley Grange, 11:45 a.m. to carry out investigation noted below."

"It's not quite conclusive," said Guy, thinking aloud.

"What do you mean 'not quite conclusive'? I couldn't be much more definite, could I?"

"No, sir. What I mean is that it doesn't quite let her out from having been at Melchester earlier. The suitcase was put in the train before 11:30, so whoever did it, if they traveled by car, had time to get back to the Grange and slip in by the back door before you went upstairs. Elspeth's alibi is that she was doing out a cupboard upstairs at the time of your visit."

"That's right! And that was after I had taken down particulars and been out to see the bed in the garden."

Guy made some mental calculations. "That would make it not earlier than twelve. There seems to be no doubt that she did out the cupboard; both the Miss Cathcarts remember seeing her."

"And so do I, though I didn't happen to make a note in my book. Both Miss Cathcarts, you say? Yes, the younger one joined us when I went out to the lawn."

"And that would be much before twelve?"

Dawes thought. "No, a few minutes after rather than before. That looks like being another spoke in our man's wheel."

"It's fortunate you noticed the time."

"There's not much that escapes me. Now about that inquest . . ."

But then the telephone rang. Dawes raised the receiver, made a few notes on his pad, and rang off.

"They're on to Willoughby at last: Warburton Private Hotel, Monk Street, just off the Cromwell Road, Earl's Court end. If you hurry, Northeast, and give tea a miss, you'll catch the five-thirty; but mind you're back in the morning in time for the inquest."

Guy started, "But . . ." and then remembered you mustn't question an order. If "our man" was Forbes, why send him off on a wild goose chase? If he got up early and came down with the milk, he ought to have an hour in Melchester in the morning to complete his case before the inquest opened. So he said, "Yes, sir," and from the door, "I'll be seeing you tomorrow."

Guy gave tea a miss and had time to do his business with the ticket collector before he settled back in the corner of his empty smoker to marshal the facts of his case. But disappointment awaited him in London. Captain Willoughby had gone out to a show and had left word that he and his wife would not be back till morning as they'd probably feel like a spot of dancing.

SATURDAY

GUY ROSE EARLY. There was a dewy freshness even about the Cromwell Road, but the Warburton Private Hotel had a permanently end-of-day appearance and smelt strongly of mice. Captain and Mrs. Willoughby had a suite on the first floor and, because they had been out late, were having breakfast upstairs and, if the gentleman would wait in the lounge, the manageress would take up his name.

Guy waited under a palm and presently he was conducted up a flight of stairs decorated with steel engravings depicting the domestic felicity of Queen Victoria and Albert the Good. In a square sitting room of immense height, a short, foxy, fortyish man in a checked suit and a young blonde lady in a pink dressing gown were finishing their breakfast of bacon and eggs. Cheerily, they welcomed him in.

"Thought you'd dig me out," said Willoughby, helping himself to marmalade. "Knew it as soon as I saw that poor old Delia Cathcart had been put down."

Guy asked why he hadn't come forward in response to the police appeal. "You don't know my wife," said Willoughby. "If I'd broken covert, she'd have got hold of me again. Tenacious woman, Gerda. A real octopus. I'm always anxious to oblige the police, but Pip and I talked it over and decided it wouldn't do."

Pip helped herself to a banana.

"That's right. Mickey came all over highbrow and talked about his communal responsibility, but we couldn't risk Gerda. You really ought to meet her, Mr. East . . . West . . ."

"Northeast. I *have* met her. Captain Willoughby, can you account for your movements on the evening of last Friday and Saturday morning up to twelve noon?"

"Good God," said Willoughby, " you don't mean to say that you've got anything on me? I hardly knew the old girl. She used to ride on my tail and she'd see me home if she could, but heavens alive, man, that kind's not my cup of tea."

Considering Pip, with her green eyes, mop of curls and thin, heart-shaped face, Guy believed him. "All the same, sir, I should like an account of your movements. We're questioning all Miss Cathcart's friends with the object of eliminating those that don't matter, and you must admit that it is impossible for us to overlook the fact that you and Miss Cathcart disappeared from your homes on the same day."

"Disgusting minds the police have," grumbled Willoughby. "Me and Delia Cathcart! Might as well have gone away with my old gray mare! Well, Inspector, this is the best I can do for you. Friday night—bridge at the Hall till eleven or so; then home. Didn't disturb Gerda; we've separate bedrooms—have for years. Didn't go to bed but packed and started in the cold light of dawn. Garaged the car. Got some breakfast at the coffee stall in the station yard. Traveled up by the 7:30, and Pip, bless her, met me at Waterloo."

"Will anyone bear you out?"

"The garage attendant and the man at the coffee stall, I should think."

"Did you travel up with anyone you knew?"

"Good God, no; not known on workmen's trains."

"And Miss . . . er . . . Pip. Can you prove that you were in London on Saturday morning?"

Pip blinked her green eyes. "Curious, aren't you? I . . . I breakfasted with the girl I've been sharing a flat with and then went to Waterloo to meet Mickey."

"Quite! And the address of your flat?"

"3, Daphne Buildings, Dean Street, off the King's Road."

Guy made a note of the address. "One last question—do you happen to remember what you were wearing that morning?"

"Scarlet and white checked skirt, scarlet jacket, no hat and white shoes."

"Thank you." Guy closed his notebook. "I suppose I can count on you to be here for a few days longer?"

"Till the end of the month," said Willoughby. "Paid the rent in advance."

Guy refused a whiskey and soda, promised not to give the address away to Mrs. Willoughby, and rushed off to catch his train. By eleven o'clock he was reporting to Dawes. "Willoughby's got an alibi of sorts, but it'll take some checking."

"There's no need to waste time on him. Forbes is our man. While you've been enjoying the sights of London, I've picked up a real clue. Two nights ago, at the Basket Makers' Arms, Forbes paid for a round of drinks with one of Miss Cathcart's notes."

"Oh!" Guy stood silent for a moment. Then, "Not traced any of the others?"

"Yes, there's another. Given in at a garage in Great Hitherford, in payment for a can of petrol, by a lady who'd had a breakdown."

"A lady?" Guy could have embraced the Superintendent. "Did they note the number?"

"Couldn't; they didn't see it. She'd run out of petrol and walked to the garage."

"Damn!"

"If she's one of Forbes' fancy ladies, we'll soon pick her up."

"She can wait, anyhow," said Guy, moving towards the door. "I've got a couple of calls to make before the inquest. The public library and—where is Giles' Square?"

"Second turn to the left after the library. But what's the idea?"

Guy, however, had rushed out and was careful not to see the Chief Constable's Daimler nor to hear the peremptory summons from its horn. A few minutes later, rudely interrupting a discussion on moss-stitch, which a young female librarian was carrying on with a matron in search of a nice love story, he was told where to find the encyclopedia. COLE to DAMA. Licking his thumb, he rapidly flicked over the pages until he came to the article he wanted. *Anomalous di*—what a mouthful! . . . ah, this was better . . . *represents the most common form, being a characteristic of about four percent of males and one-tenth of this proportion of females* . . . one-tenth of four percent—an outside chance, but outsiders sometimes came home. . . .

* * * *

"What a dreadful bare little room," said Nancy. "And, darling, how cold!"

"I'm glad I had the sense to put on my coat," said Mrs. Hemmings. "Jess, girl, you must be frozen in them short sleeves."

"I'm shivering," said Sheila, "but I suppose that's nerves."

"It's trembling, Miss," said Jessie. "I've nothing to fear, but my legs are all of a shake. Is this where they locks people up?"

"No," said Elspeth. "This is just a waiting room for witnesses. Would you like my coat, Miss Sheila? I'm quite warm."

"No, thank you," said Sheila rather coldly. "You'd better all sit down, if there are enough chairs."

Taylor said, "Seeing as we're witnesses and not criminals, they might of given us something better than 'orse-'air to sit on. It's apt to strike cold."

"You should wear more," said Mrs. Hemmings unsympathetically.

Jessie began, "Will any of us be wanted in court, Miss? I do 'ope not. I've nothing to 'ide, but all the same I don't fancy it, some'ow. Don't know what you won't catch, either. . . ." She broke off as the door opened and a rat-faced girl walked in, looking here and there and everywhere with her bright, shifty brown eyes.

Sylvia Smallbone had been persuaded by Guy to join his party, just to sit in a waiting room for half an hour or so with some other ladies. He had made it right with the management of the Red Lion and he had promised Sylvia that it would be to her advantage and that when it was over he would explain the idea. Sylvia was feeling important. She shot a disdainful glance at the party already in possession. None of them was so stylishly dressed as she was in her mauve jumper, mauve halo hat, and gray flannel coat and skirt.

Scarcely had Miss Smallbone seated herself than the door opened again and, dressed dramatically in black and orange, Gerda Willoughby strode into the room. "Oh, Miss Cathcart . . . and Nancy . . . I'm so sorry. I'm sure that in your great grief you don't want to be bothered by me, but I was told that I must come. I can't *think* why they want me. I don't know anything about your poor sister, but I feel that perhaps I ought to have taken legal advice, only solicitors are so sordid and everything's so simple and nothing's ugly if you just bare your soul. So I thought, well, that's what I shall do if I have to answer any question: just bare my soul."

Sheila said, "I wonder why they wanted you to come. Of course that Northeast man isn't very intelligent. . . ."

"Oh, don't you think so? I've had some *thrilling* conversations with him. We discussed Time. . . ."

She was interrupted by the appearance of a stocky blue-eyed middle-aged man. He said, "Excuse me, ladies," and, taking pains not to trip over anyone's feet, he stepped across the room and stood with his back to the fireplace. He remained there for about five minutes. Then he sighed heavily, said, "Excuse me, ladies," and left the room, stepping as carefully as when he had come in.

"I wonder who that was?" said Nancy.

"Another witness, I expect," said Mrs. Willoughby. "He struck me as a typical member of the lower middle class, quite cancerous with respectability. As he stood there by the fireplace I could see right into his twisted little soul."

"I wonder why he went away," said Nancy.

"Oh, he'll come back in a minute," said Mrs. Willoughby. "I expect he's just gone to see a man about a dog—men always do."

But the stocky man didn't come back. The next person to enter the room was a tall constable, who told Sheila that she was wanted in court.

Sheila leapt to her feet and stumbled out, kicking Miss Smallbone on the ankle and treading on Taylor's corn. Taylor drew in her breath and Miss Smallbone muttered, "Clumsy thing!" Then there was silence. Jessie stared at Miss Smallbone. Miss Smallbone stared at the dirty mark which Sheila's shoe had left on her art silk stocking. Nancy twisted her fingers. Gerda Willoughby gazed at a shaft of sunlight. Elspeth sat like a statue. Mrs. Hemmings snuffled and Taylor, vainly striving to stifle the gurglings of her gastric juices, from time to time murmured, "Pardon me."

And presently the door opened and Sheila stood there again. She had taken off her glasses and was wiping them with her pocket handkerchief. She said, "I was only wanted to give evidence of identification. The inquest is adjourned for a week and now we can all go home."

"What—aren't none of us wanted?" said Mrs. Hemmings in a bitterly disappointed tone.

"Not today. The police are so inconsiderate!"

"Never mind," said Gerda Willoughby. "Of course, it's been horribly sordid, but it'll make us more sensitive to beauty, so in a way, you see, it's been good for our souls. I feel terribly hurt—ugliness does hurt me terribly—and I'm going to rush off now to be healed by flowers and trees and birds."

She rushed. Nancy turned to Sheila. "Was it very dreadful, darling?"

"Not as dreadful as I expected. I was only asked if I had identified the body and when Delia was last seen alive and if she was in good health and whether she often slept out—I think that was all. Inspector Northeast described how he found Delia and Doctor Baker gave some medical evidence, which was rather horrible. None of the jury asked any questions. I suppose next week there'll be more."

"Didn't they say anything about suspecting anyone?"

"No, darling. I suppose they'll bring that up next week."

"Oh, dear. How slow they are!"

"What does it matter?" said Sheila wearily. "Nothing they do can bring Delia back to us again. Let's go now, darling. I want to get away from here."

* * * *

"Well, that went off all right," said the Chief Constable. "We may be old-fashioned down here, Inspector, but we have got a coroner who knows how to do what he's told."

"That's right, sir," corroborated the Superintendent. "And it won't take us a week to get our man. We've just got a little tidying to do."

Guy said, "Excuse me, sir, I want to put through one telephone call. Then I think we shall have all the evidence we need."

Both men stared at him.

"All right. You won't be long?"

"No, sir. It's only a local call. I'll come along to the Superintendent's office."

Guy left them to go into a telephone kiosk and the Chief Constable said, "Mysterious feller! Has he got something up his sleeve, do you think?"

"He may have. I advised him this morning to concentrate on Forbes."

While the two men waited at the station, conversation languished. Dawes sat like a graven image, but the Chief Constable beat an impatient tattoo on the table, cleared his throat and twice turned round to glance at the loudly ticking clock on the mantelpiece. He had opened his mouth to make some remark, when Guy came in, grinning.

Carruthers glared at him, and the grin vanished. "Now, Northeast, let's hear what you've been up to."

Guy was rather pleased with himself and, in a hurry to receive their compliments, thoughtlessly began, "The idea really came to me over a glass of beer at the Dog and Duck."

He saw the two men exchange a glance and he went on quickly. "I was there . . . er . . . primarily on business. You may remember, sir, that we agreed I should concentrate on alibis or the time the suitcase was planted in the train. Before going out to Marley, I called at the cafe where Jessie and Funge had their 'elevens' on the Saturday morning, and the waitress, who had attended on them, supplied them with a cast iron alibi. My next job was to check up Ames' movements . . ."

Dawes interrupted, "But it was a woman who planted the suitcase. Ames isn't a woman, Northeast."

"No, sir," Guy said patiently. "But I had to see if I could eliminate him. I discovered that he had been playing in the final of the village darts competition at the critical time on the Saturday morning. So Ames was apparently out."

"Not very close reasoning, Northeast," said Major Carruthers. "If he had a female accomplice he might have handed over the suitcase to her whenever he wanted."

"Granted, sir. I didn't rule him out finally." Guy couldn't resist a sly glance at Dawes as he added, "I realized that I must still keep an open mind. I ordered . . . er . . . a snack and pondered again over my chart and I found myself asking, Mr. X, why did you make that mistake? If murderers never made mistakes they'd never be caught. I studied the marks I had given for the likelihood of making that mistake in packing the clothes. Could a woman have put in garments that not only didn't match but positively shrieked? A woman had planted the suitcase, but I had marked all the woman suspects as unlikely to make the mistake. What had I missed?"

He paused for a moment. The Superintendent's cold eyes were skeptical. The Chief Constable was studying his nails.

"Pondering over this point," Guy went on, "I drove to the Grange to check up the housemaid's alibi. By this time I had reason to believe that she was married to Forbes. . . ."

"What's that? You never mentioned that point to me."

Guy badly wanted to get a bit of his own back by pointing out that, if the Chief Constable had allowed him to outline the reasoning on which the marks shown on the chart had been awarded, he would have been aware of the suspicions against Elspeth. But you did yourself no good by scoring off those who were in authority over you, so he said, "I only established the relationship yesterday."

"H'm. You're not exactly cooperative, Northeast."

"I'm sorry, sir. I questioned Elspeth closely as to her movements on Saturday morning and then, so as to confirm her statement, I asked if I might have a word with the Miss Cathcarts. When I went into the drawing room, Miss Nancy was doing needlework and she was surrounded by skeins of colored wool, just like those they used when I joined the Force, as a test for colorblindness. A colorblind woman could have packed that suitcase. . . ."

"Rather farfetched, what?"

"Still, it explained a lot that had been mysterious before, sir. I don't know whether you've studied colorblindness and Mendelism, but I used to dabble with sweet peas, and I'd read the subject up. I had an idea that colorblindness was a male complaint, transmitted from one generation to another through the female. My whole theory crashed if women couldn't themselves be colorblind. From the Miss Cathcarts I got the address of a Melchester oculist, but, before bothering him, I checked up in the encyclopedia and found that one-tenth of four percent of women are colorblind."

With a groan of impatience, the Superintendent got to his feet. He addressed himself to the Chief Constable. "Don't you think we'd better bring Forbes inside, sir, and leave these scientific details till later?"

Guy said gently, "But Forbes isn't our man."

"Then who is?"

"It's a woman."

"His wife?

"No, sir."

"But, damn it all, Northeast, you've just been proving it is."

"No, sir. I've deduced that a colorblind woman packed the suit-case." He paused for effect. "And my suspect was identified by the ticket collector at a parade I arranged this morning."

Dawes spluttered. "You held an identification parade? Where?"

"In the waiting room at the Coroner's Court. I had all our female suspects and one or two 'supers' for luck, and Janes spotted her at once. She had ample opportunity to commit the murder, to pack and plant the suitcase and, being colorblind—I've just verified that over the phone by consulting her oculist—she is unable to distinguish darkish greens from reds and browns. I must admit I can't fathom the motive. A woman's motive is often obscure, but we'll get on to that later."

"Well—let's know who it is."

Guy told them. The Chief Constable's red face darkened to crimson. Guy slowly marshaled his evidence; she had been picked by the ticket collector out of a party of seven; no one had better opportunity of committing the murder, packing the suitcase and planting it in the train; no woman with a normal color sense would have packed a brown dress, green shoes and a red evening bag.

The Chief Constable slumped in his chair. "Good God," he muttered. "Good God!" Dawes, convinced and a little subdued, said, "We'd better be moving out to the Grange."

Carruthers said, "Yes, yes. You fellers start. My Daimler will soon overhaul you." He passed his hand over his eyes and added in a low voice, very unlike his normal one, "A nasty business at any time, but when it's one of your friends . . . ." He left the sentence unfinished.

Dawes and Guy went out. Carruthers got wearily to his feet, walked across the room and looked out of the window. He looked at a yellow brick wall, but he didn't see it. He saw a dismal street and the rain falling and he heard a prison clock striking the hour.

He walked back to the table and beat a tattoo on it. Women were different. Ineradicably he believed that. All his life he had given up his seat to ladies, opened doors for them, picked up their handkerchiefs; his mind connected them with the softer side of life, with flowers and firesides, children, chintzes and caresses—all wrong that the dainty gentle creatures should vote, earn, rule, or . . . be hanged. All wrong. Well, he'd stop it. His mind made up, he wasn't the man to hesitate. He reached for the telephone receiver and gave the number of Marley Grange. . . .

* * * *

Fifteen minutes later, Dawes and Guy, in the police car, arrived at the Grange. The day was cloudless; on the brown roof of the stable the fantails were cooing; waiting at the front door, Guy was once again conscious of the smell of hay. Taylor admitted them. "The Miss Cathcarts?" said Dawes, and Taylor answered, "Yes, sir; they're at home," and ushered the two men towards the drawing room.

Guy said, "We'll find our way," and stepped past her. He opened the drawing-room door and the Superintendent heard him say, "Oh," and then, "Is your sister in? There are one or two questions that I'd like to put to her."

"She's in her bedroom, I think. She was called to the telephone and then she went upstairs. Shall I . . . ."

"It's all right," Guy said. "I'll go up." He shut the door quickly and turned towards the stairs.

"Why not have her fetched down?" whispered Dawes.

"Listen!" said Guy. The house was very quiet, but somewhere upstairs a dog was whining and scratching at a door. Guy didn't wait for the Superintendent's comment. Taking two steps in a stride, he ran upstairs.

The door, at which the dog was whining, wouldn't open. Guy shook it with no effect, and turned to Dawes.

"Better get permission, sir. . . ."

The Superintendent went downstairs, spoke at the drawing-room door, and called up, "Carry on." Guy put his shoulder to the door, the lock gave, and he stumbled into the room.

It was full of sunshine. The window was open and the curtains were blowing in the breeze. On the floor near the writing table lay Nancy Cathcart. The sunshine fell brightly on her graying hair.

Guy knelt down beside her. She was dead.

He touched her right hand. It was warm and the second finger was stained with ink, not yet dry.

Then in the doorway Sheila Cathcart screamed.

Guy got up from his knees, but Dawes was supporting Sheila from the room, and talking fatuously but kindly about sparing her mother and looking on the bright side. One of the maids must have come running upstairs, for Guy heard Dawes say, "Take care of her," and then he came back into the room. "Well," he said, "we were too late, it seems."

"Yes, sir. But I can't say I'm altogether sorry," said Guy.

Dawes was looking down at Nancy. "It doesn't do to be soft," he said, as though arguing with himself. "But, look here, Inspector, how did she guess we were after her? Did you give it away?"

Guy was standing at the writing table. A book lay open there. The ink was fresh on the page and the last sentences were smudged as though by a trailing hand. He said, "Here you are, sir—Miss Nancy's diary. I fancy it will give us the whole story, cut and dried."

* * * *

Up there, in the tragic sunlit bedroom, with Dawes reading over his shoulder and breathing down the back of his neck, Guy could only glance quickly through the final pages of Nancy Cathcart's diary; but, later on, as he sat in the lounge at the Red Lion with a long drink untouched beside him, he read through that heart-rending record of a long domestic tyranny. At what period of her life Nancy had first begun to hate her sister, he never knew; already in the January of the year she had written, "Of course D. has found out about the Christmas presents I gave the Appleyard children. She said she shouldn't have thought that I would have spent so much on them. I said nothing, but felt like throwing my plate at her." Later in

January: "D. said I ought to start driving the big car again. Refused.
D. laughed and said, 'Poor baby!' Poor baby! If she knew how I feel
sometimes! If she knew what I used to feel like, driving that car with
her sitting beside me and telling me what to do. God, how I hate
her!" Then, "D. says I ought to take up golf. I won't. I won't." And,
"D. on about golf again. Why should I take it up when I don't want
to?" Then in February: "D.'s been nagging and nagging about my
taking up golf, and I've given in as usual. She's kindly presented me
with some of her rusty old clubs and I've got to start tomorrow. Why
does she always get her way? Why do we all give in to her? She
doesn't order us about but it's that awful 'I should have thought' and
'I shouldn't have thought' and 'what a funny idea' and 'fancy.'" Then,
the next day, "D. came home and told funny stories about my golf.
She's funny enough herself—she gets more like a horse every day,
but no one tells funny stories about her." In April the golf was apparently given up, for, "D. said that she could understand people not
being able to hit a ball well, but she couldn't understand people not
being able to hit a ball at all. S. stood up to her, but was soon squashed
and Mother burbled her usual piece about niches." In May there
had been trouble of another kind. "Poor darling John keeps on
being sick and D. says it's because I overfeed him. She wouldn't have
thought that I would have given him that fish last night. Damn her,
he's my dog, mine, mine. Mother got worried—I believe it was only
because of the carpets—and when D. was out, S. telephoned for the
vet. It wasn't Mr. Ross who came, but his assistant. He's nice and
awfully good-looking. He gave me some pills for John and said he
would call again in the morning. When D. came home she said we
had panicked and that a tablespoon of castor oil was all John had
needed."

And the next day: "Vet came again. He's marvelous. I think he's
my ideal. His name is Forbes and the initials on his bag are D.F., so
his Christian name may be Derek, or Denis, or David. I do hope it's
David. I shall call him David to myself, but it will be awful if it slips
out while I'm talking to him."

A few days later, John was sick again. "D. said it was my fault for
giving him a teeny bit of chocolate. Mother said I'd better telephone
the vet, so I did and David's lovely deep voice answered. He said he
would come at once, and, after a bit, he did, and when we were
looking at John his hand touched mine and I'm sure he meant it.
Just after that D. came in and spoilt everything, asking awful questions about John's bowels, etc. No one will ever fall in love with *her,*

that's one thing. After David had gone, D. said he looked like a dancing partner. I could have *killed* her."

For the next few weeks there were only brief references to Delia. "D. doesn't like my new dress." "D. said she could see a lot of gray in my hair." "D. went out for a ride and insisted on taking John with her. I waited in agonies, thinking she might let him get run over." "D.'s got a beastly new patent breakfast food and says we all ought to eat it. I wish it would poison her." "D. fell off Flavia. Ha, ha. I wish I had seen her." "Damn it, I've got a horrid spot on my chin and of course as soon as D. came down to breakfast she passed remarks about it." "D.'s gone to the dentist. I hope he hurts her." Then, in June: "D. has sent for the vet about Sultan. Will Mr. Ross come or my own dear David? But Forbes came, and I watched out of the spare room window. David looked more marvelous than ever, and presently I plucked up courage and went downstairs trying to think of an excuse to go across to the stable. At last I thought of taking John with me and asking David if he looked in better condition. So I did. D. said, 'Oh, your fat dog's all right,' but David patted John and said that he was a good old fellow and lucky to have such a kind missus. D. was annoyed and said sharply, 'Well, it's the horse you've come to see,' but David took no notice of her and said he could see that I loved animals. D. was furious, and after David had gone, she said he was tipsy. When I said he wasn't, she laughed and said I was an innocent little thing. Why should I always be treated as though I were a child? I'm a woman of thirty-eight and that's just the age when you're capable of real passion. To men of experience a young girl's love is like milk and water."

Two days later the fat was in the fire. "D. says that David ordered the wrong treatment for Sultan. She says he was drunk and didn't know what he was doing, and she's going to write to Mr. Ross and complain about him. Now the beast has telephoned for him. . . . David came and I watched out of the spare room window. D. went on at him. She was furious and talked and talked with her head nodding. David very calm and noble. They went into the stable and then I couldn't see anything. I couldn't take John out to them again, so I went out to my car and opened the bonnet and pretended to be looking at the carburetor. Presently David came out of the stable. I wanted to say a few words of comfort to him, but I couldn't think how to begin, so I just said, 'Good morning.' David didn't answer, but went to his car and drove off looking angry. Perhaps he didn't hear me—my voice isn't like D.'s, but soft and seductive—but I think it was really because he's too strong a man to seek for comfort in anyone. I'm glad he's strong, but it's awful to witness a strong man's anguish and not to be able to do anything."

The next day: "D. keeps on about David. If she does write to Mr. Ross, I wonder if I could intercept the letter. That would be something that I could do for David. I nearly stood up for him today at lunch—I don't know why I didn't, only there's something about D. which makes it impossible. I don't know what it is. If I look straight at her when she's looking at me, it makes my eyes water. I wonder if it's the same with S. Sometimes she stands up to D. and they have an argument. It's always D. who wins, but S. doesn't seem to mind—I suppose her music is the only thing she really cares about. She's sexless, too. Not like me. I'm capable of feeling and inspiring a great enduring passion. I wonder whether John Owen ever thinks of me. I'm sure he would have proposed if I'd met him again, and Mother would have asked him to our picnic if D. hadn't said he was common. D. has spoilt my life. I might have hunted and met men that way, if she hadn't made me ride those awful ponies and then said I was nervous. I'm not nervous. I'm just as capable of heroic acts as she is. Why do we all treat her as the dashing one of the family?"

A few days passed with entries you might have found in any quiet countrywoman's diary. Then came: "Gardened for a bit, but D. came out and showed me how to do it. She said, 'Get out of my way, you silly darling, and I'll show you.' I didn't get out of the way, but she just pushed past me and knelt down beside the border. I had been ever so happy gardening and thinking how lovely it would be to have a little home of my own and make the garden nice for a tired man to sit in on summer evenings, and I simply boiled with rage. While D. was kneeling there I could see a bit of her red scraggy neck between the short stiff black hairs at the back of her head and her horrid high collar and I thought how I'd like to take hold of her neck and squeeze the life out of her. It would be lovely if she was dead. Think of waking up and knowing that all day you could do as you liked and there'd be no one to say, 'Fancy stuffing indoors,' or, 'You don't want that thick scarf on,' or 'What a funny idea to go to church on a weekday!' Why *should* she stop me doing what I want? Yesterday I'd have bought that green and red material for my new frock only I *knew* she'd say, 'What crude colors,' so I got a wishy-washy thing that no one will know from my old one. Why shouldn't I wear what I like? It's my own body."

From that date onwards there was scarcely a day when some

domineering act of Delia's was not recorded. "Wet all day. I should
have liked a fire in the evening and I'm sure Mother and S. would
have been glad of one too, but D. said that we couldn't be cold—she
wasn't. Just because I missed brushing John yesterday, D. did it. She
said, 'There, poor old man, now you've had a real good grooming.'
I stood watching her. I expect she thought I was doing what she calls
'picking up wrinkles,' but really I was thinking how I hate her. I do
hate her. I don't only hate her mind but I hate her body. I hate the
back of her neck where it shows between her hair and her collar. I
hate her brown thin hands and the shape of her nails. I hate her
hard, gray eyes, that make mine water, and I hate the two bristly
hairs that have begun to show at the corners of her upper lip. I wish
she would get ill and die, but she never will. I know I shall die first. I
shall die and be buried and never know what life could have been
like without her."

There came a day in late June. "D. has been given tickets for
Wimbledon. I don't know how she gets them out of people, but I
suppose she nags and nags until they send them. I should like to go,
but D. says I don't like watching tennis. I never go anywhere. D. says
I'm shy, but I'm not—if I go to a party and she's there I can't talk
because I know that afterwards she'll say, 'Fancy your telling Mrs. So-
and-so what we pay for the house at Southwold,' or, 'Darling, everybody isn't as interested in your fat dog as you are.' It was she who
first said I was the home bird, and now Mother's always saying it. I
don't want to be a home bird. If it hadn't been for D. I could have
had lots of friends, but whenever I make friends with anybody, she
says they are boring or common. Last year when I gave some wind-
falls to that nice Mrs. Smith for her dear little children, D. said we
didn't want to get mixed up with people who lived in bungalows. In
every way she's spoilt my life, and she'll go on spoiling it until I'm
dead and buried.

"*June 28th*. A dull day, but I suppose it was no duller than usual.
Had breakfast early just because D. wanted to school Flavia before
starting for Wimbledon. Brushed John. Walked round the garden
and saw D. schooling Flavia in the paddock. Flavia reared so high I
thought she was going to fall over backwards. I wish she had. I wish
she had fallen on the top of D. and crushed all the breath out of her
body. Sometimes I think that nothing could kill D. I'm sure no poison would. If you put poison in her coffee, she'd drink it and then
you'd wait and wait and nothing would happen. If you tried to suffo-
cate her, you'd creep into her bedroom at night and put a pillow

over her head and press and press and press, but when you took the pillow away, she'd be just as much alive as ever. The only way to kill her would be to hit her with something sharp—an axe or a hatchet. That would go through her skull all right and you'd see the blood come and then you'd know for certain that she was dead or dying. What awful thoughts I have, but I do so hate her. She came home from Wimbledon and told us all about it and what was wrong with everybody's play and what strokes they should have made—I wonder she isn't a champion. In case she should look at me and say, 'Why is our baby so silent?' I asked if she had seen any pretty frocks, and she said it was tennis, not frocks that she went to look at. I hate D. I *hate* D. I HATE HER.

"*June* 29th. I was late for breakfast. I couldn't sleep last night. I lay awake and thought of D. and of all the years I've got to go on living with her. I suppose that one day Mother will die and D. and S. and I will just go on living together. I've got my own money—I could go away but I shall never be able to. Last year I made up my mind to tell them I wanted to go and I decided what I should say, but one day after another passed and I couldn't say it. I shall never be free while D.'s alive and I *know* she'll live longer than I shall. Today, she was more hateful than ever. She went on at Elspeth about a cobweb and the poor girl did look so upset and helpless. I should have liked to have said something nice to her, but I knew it would get round to D. somehow. I'm sure the maids hate D. I wish one of them would murder her. I often feel like murdering her, only it would be awful to be hanged—still, I'm not sure I wouldn't rather be dead than go on living with D. bossing me forever and ever.

"*Later. A* dreadfully dull evening. I cut out my wishy-washy material, and tacked it, and wished I had had the red and green. D. wouldn't have the wireless on, though I wanted it dreadfully. Someone was going to sing *You Are My Heart's Delight*, and I do love it—it makes me think of David. Instead, I made up a story about how I killed D. and nobody ever found out who did it. I don't believe anyone would find out a murder that was planned by an educated person. Most murderers are rough men like farm laborers and they're caught because they do something absolutely half-witted, like strangling girls with mufflers that everybody knows belong to them. If I murdered D. I wouldn't make any silly mistakes like that, and I'm sure no one would think of suspecting the little home bird. It would be lovely to kill D.—she'd be so surprised to find that silly timid me had the power to send brave competent her right out of the world forever. Oh, that's a lovely idea! For years and years she's bossed me, but I should turn the tables on her and she'd never be able to do anything about it—never. She'd be dead and buried and the worms would eat her wonderful marvelous D. I think I shall kill her. To-night in bed I shall think out a really clever way.

"*June 30th*, Last night I lay awake and thought of a plan. It's so clever that I'm sure no one will ever find it out. D. is sleeping in the garden every night now, and I shall kill her there and, somehow or another, I shall hide her body. Then I shall creep back into the house and pack some of her clothes in that ugly new rawhide suitcase she's so proud of, and I shall put it in my car—in the boot under the back seat, where nobody ever looks, and next morning, when everybody's fussing and wondering where darling Delia is, I shall drive to Melches-ter Station and buy a ticket for London and put the suitcase on the rack in an empty carriage, and everyone will be quite sure that D. traveled up to London and just forgot it when she got out of the train at Waterloo. Now comes a bit of my plan that's especially clever. Of course, D. would have traveled in clothes of some sort, so I shall take her blue flowered frock and the hat and shoes she wears with it and throw them away somewhere, and the lucky thing is that she bossed me into getting a blue outfit something like it, so I shall wear that myself and, if the silly police are called in, they'll be absolutely done, because the porters and people on the platform will remember see-ing a lady in blue carrying a rawhide suitcase. Of course I shan't be so silly as to go *off* the platform the way I went *on*—I shall go down the subway. As well as buying a ticket for London, I shall get a plat-form ticket out of a machine, which I shall give up to the man in the subway. *Memo.* I mustn't forget to throw away D.'s dark blue hand-bag.

"I think this is a wonderful plan. Last night I couldn't see a flaw in it, but when I woke up this morning, I did see one. Supposing that when I've killed D. I find I can't move her body? She's small and light, of course, but I'm not very strong; I'm not horrible and man-nish like D., or huge and clumsy like S. I'm an appealing feminine type, and that's why strong men like David are attracted to me. Well, this day passed, and I really don't know what we did, because all the time I was thinking hard—oh, wouldn't they have been surprised if they had known what their 'baby' and their 'home bird' was think-ing! It makes me laugh out loud, but I mustn't, because D. has just come up to get ready for bed and she might hear me and come into my room—without knocking, of course—and say, 'Fancy laughing when you're all alone in your bedroom.' Well, I thought and thought and at last I got it. D's always fussing about the maids and their young men, so, as soon as she has said good night to me, I shall creep out into the garden and hide behind the stable. Then, when she's been in bed for a few minutes, I shall give one of those whistles that the village boys call after their girls with. I think I can do it, but I daren't try now. Tomorrow I shall go out in my car and practice. When D. hears it, she's sure to get up and come to see who it is—she's so interfering. I shall stand up on the midden just behind the corner of the stable and I shall have the hatchet out of the woodshed in my hands and I shall bring it down on her head as she comes round the corner. The hatchet will split her head open and I shall see the blood and know that she's dead and I'm free to say what I like and do what I like and wear what I like forever. Then I shall pull poor limp dead D. on the midden and heap some straw on her and the next day Ames will put some more straw on, and every day she'll be buried deeper and I'll be safer. It's a lovely plan. I can't see a single flaw in it."

On the page where the events of July 1st should have been recorded, Nancy had written only the one word—"Successful." Then, on July 2nd: "Last night was the first night for years when I didn't write in my diary, but it was no use writing *before* and *afterwards* I wasn't so silly as to turn my light on. But now Mother has gone to bed crying—she doesn't realize that with D. gone she won't be bossed off to bed at ten o'clock every evening, but she'll be able to stay up as long as she likes and finish what she's reading even if it does mean that she'll have nothing to read tomorrow—and S. has gone to bed with watery eyes and a red nose—she doesn't realize that she can have the piano turned round now, and that no one will say, 'Well, come on, spit it out,' when she stammers. At last I'm alone and I've turned on *both* the lights and there's no one to say I'm extravagant; and I've shut the window *top and bottom* and there's no one to say it's unhealthy. Ha, ha, D.! You're dead, you're deaf, you're dumb, you're blind, and already I've started to do the things you wouldn't let me do—you don't know that after dinner I brought John up to my bedroom and LET HIM SIT ON THE BED and gave him a WHOLE BAR of chocolate!!

"Well, I must go back to last night. All evening D. was as bossy as usual—we all got told off for feeding Flavia—she wouldn't have thought that I would have given my old orange frock to Jessie— Mother must sack Jessie—she couldn't think why S. and I don't sleep

in the garden—I ought to take more exercise—it was Mother's bedtime. And then, when I was going to let John out, she insisted on
doing it. Ordinarily, I should have been boiling with rage, but I just
sat and sewed and thought of all the evenings to come when she'd be
dead and her mouth shut forever. I went to bed and when she came
in to say good night—later than usual because she'd been downstairs bullying poor little Jessie—I pretended to be half-asleep, but,
as soon as she was safely in her room, I jumped up and put on my
dark dressing gown. I crept downstairs and into the garden. John
was in his basket in the lobby, but I told him to lie still and tomorrow
I would give him lots of chocolate. I tiptoed down to the woodshed
and got the hatchet and then I crouched on the stable side of the yew
hedge and watched through a hole I made until I saw D. come out. I
waited for ten minutes by my wristwatch and then I whistled. Nothing happened and I was terrified that I'd waited too long and she was
fast asleep and wouldn't hear me. I whistled again and then, thank
goodness, I heard her bed creak. I slipped back to my place by the
midden and held the hatchet ready and after ages and ages I heard
her footsteps, soft and shuffling because of her bedroom slippers.
She seemed to be wandering round the stable yard, so I whistled
again quite softly, and the next thing I really *knew* was that D. was
lying at my feet—*my* feet—and there was a wound in her head out of
which a little blood had oozed, but now she wasn't bleeding. I did
wish that she was—for one horrid moment I thought she couldn't be
dead, but then I felt her heart and it had stopped beating. I could
have danced with joy. I remember hearing myself say out loud, 'Ha,
ha, D. Now you're only a silly dead body!' and it was the easiest thing
in the world to move some of the straw and pull her up on the
midden. Her slippers fell off, but I put them on again, and then I
heaped the straw over her. Of course I wasn't so silly as to leave my
fingerprints on the pitchfork. When all that was done, I wiped my
fingerprints off the hatchet too, and with my hanky wrapped round
it, I pushed it down the stable drain, where no one will think of
looking for it. Then I crept back to the house, let myself in with my
latchkey, and tiptoed up the stairs. I mayn't be good at silly old games
and athletics, but one of the things I can do, is to creep about quietly.
I couldn't put very much in the suitcase—you can't carry heavy things
quietly—but I put in the sort of things D. would have taken for a
night or two—her brown evening dress, brown sandals and evening
bag, etc., and I didn't forget her sponge, toothbrush and paste, as
some people might have done. I took her handbag and her blue

dress and hat and shoes and rolled them up in a piece of brown paper I had ready in my dressing-gown pocket, and I'd been clever enough to think of another thing—a weight off the kitchen scales to make the parcel sink—I had planned to throw it into a pond I know of, on the way to Melchester. I had to be awfully careful going downstairs, but fortunately the carpet's a very thick one. I hurried out to my garage—I call it a garage but of course the big car lives in the real garage and my poor little car has to put up with a horrid old shed. I put the suitcase and the parcel in the boot of my car, and then there was nothing more to do but to go to bed.

"I rather wished there *had* been something more to do—it had all been so lovely and exciting, but I consoled myself by thinking of all the clever things I should do today. I went to sleep at once and when I woke up this morning it was lovely and gave me such a peaceful feeling just to lie and think, 'No more D.' Of course, later on, there was an awful fuss. Mother soon panicked and I offered to go out in my car and look for D. Had a job with S., who offered to go, but she's easy to manage. I buzzed off and, as it was still early and there was nobody about, I took the opportunity to throw the parcel into the pond on the Melchester road. It sank beautifully. I drove round a bit, laughing and singing, and then I went back to the house— oh, dear, no sign of darling Delia! Offered to go on looking for her—wasn't it good of me?—and this time I drove into Melchester and did the station part—it went off beautifully. Drove home. Found Mother and S. on the doorstep with a great fat stupid policeman. Looked at him appealingly and told him I'd just seen a dreadful rough man, and, of course, he believed me. We all went to D.'s room and the silly policeman found out just what I meant them to, and thinks that D. had gone off on a jaunt, just as I intended! I wonder why it has taken me so long to discover how clever I am? Ha, ha, you great big policeman, you're no match for little me!"

For the next few days, this tone persisted, a crescendo of vanity sounding through the record of events. The broadcast message inspired: "Fancy, the very air's vibrating about something I've done," and it was, "Come on! The more the merrier," when Scotland Yard was called in. All the time Nancy was making the best of her newfound freedom. She bought a lipstick, presented Mrs. Smith with two huge cauliflowers, bought high-heeled shoes and sent a subscription to the Waifs and Strays. Guy bit his lip as he read, "A huge great detective has arrived from Scotland Yard. He's got lovely blue eyes, I must say, and I believe he was rather attracted to little me, but he's not the type I admire; I'm sure he doesn't know the meaning of passion—he reminds me of a stupid placid Guernsey cow. The funny thing was that I felt quite sorry for him—he won't find out anything and I expect he'll get into a row about it when he goes back to Scotland Yard."

Even the discovery of Delia's body had failed to shake Nancy's confidence. She wrote, "Rather a nuisance—today the Guernsey cow found D. and I'd thought she wouldn't be discovered at any rate until the autumn, and then only if Appleyard wanted some manure. Old Major C. came in and tried to break it gently. S. made a fuss and Mother had a heart attack. I tried to squeeze out some tears, but I couldn't, so I just sat and stared in front of me and, as the silly old fool went out, I heard him whisper to S. that I was stunned by the shock and that it would be better for me if I cried! Until all this happened, I had no idea that I was such a good actress. It comes quite naturally to me. I daresay I should have been a Duse or a Bernhardt if I had thought of going on the stage."

The publicity that the newspapers gave to the murder definitely pleased her. "To think that all this is being written about something I've done! The papers say that an early arrest is expected. I believe the Guernsey cow has been talking to the maids a lot, and Cook told S. that she thinks they suspect Ames. Well, I can't help it. Ames isn't a nice man; he smells horrid and I'm sure he doesn't lead a nice life and, anyhow, rough men like that don't feel things like we do. D. has been taken away to the mortuary. I wish I had seen her, but, of course, it was S. who was asked to identify the body; they thought it would be too upsetting for me!! I asked S. what D. looked like, and S. said, 'Very peaceful,' but I'm sure she didn't. I wonder if the worms have begun on her.

"S. and Mother have decided that we must go into mourning, so this evening a person came out from Boles and Finch's with some clothes for us to choose. It was sickening having to have black, but I chose a dress with a lovely fluffy white collar. D. would have said, 'I shouldn't have thought you would have had that Toby frill,' but you're dead now, D. . . ."

Then: "This afternoon the Guernsey cow came about the inquest. For some silly reason of his own, he wants all the maids to go. S. didn't want me to go, but luckily the cow wanted us both. I suppose the verdict will be the one about 'murder by a person or persons unknown,' and then we shall have all the bother of the funeral and then, at last, I shall be able to start my lovely new life without D. I do hope that Mother and S. won't keep up their silly sniveling much longer."

On returning from the inquest, Nancy had made a short entry: "Hooray! It's over and I didn't even have to go into court. I wonder more people don't commit murder—it's ever so easy if you've got brains. But, of course, you need courage, too. I must be awfully brave—if I had been a man I should have made a splendid soldier and probably have got the V.C. . . . ."

A few lines were left blank, and then in a shaky sprawling handwriting, very different from Nancy's normal, rather insipid copperplate, came the pages that Guy had read and wouldn't forget in years. "Oh, God help me! They must have discovered everything! A little while ago, when I was out in the garden with John, S. called and said that Major Carruthers wanted to speak to me on the telephone. I couldn't think why, and then I thought that perhaps he'd realized that I'm the cleverest of the family and wanted to ask me some quite ordinary question. I went to the 'phone and I can't remember exactly what he said, but he told me that the police are coming out here to arrest me! I couldn't believe it at first—what mistake can I have made?—but, when I did, I dropped the receiver and ran out of the room. S. was in the hall, and she started talking to me, but I pushed past her and ran upstairs and locked myself in my bedroom. I didn't panic or cry, like most women would have done, but I sat down on my bed and made up my mind what I would do. I couldn't bear to be hanged—the rope and everything would be too awful— and I soon thought of something—the doctor gave us a box of tablets for Mother—she was to take one every night to make her sleep and, even if she couldn't sleep, she was never to take more than two. S. and I have been keeping the box in the bathroom cupboard, and I've just been in there and taken twenty—one after another with lots of sips of water. Presently I shall go to sleep and then I shall die—I'm not frightened, but I think it's very sad that I should die when I've only had just these few days of life without D. She spoiled my whole life, and I think it's much worse to spoil a person's life than to kill someone; people talk a lot about freedom and how splendid it is, and all I wanted was to be free. I wonder if I shall be free when I'm dead? I'm afraid I shan't. If there is another life, D.'s there already —she'll be waiting for me. . . .

"I'm beginning to feel sleepy. It's a lovely afternoon. There's a sort of golden light over everything and the only sounds I can hear are the fantails cooing and the whir of the mowing machine. When I was in the bathroom, John came upstairs to me—he's sitting beside me now, and whenever I look down at him, he wags his tail. He's such a dear fat dog. I'm going to leave my diary out, so that everyone can read it and understand why I killed D., so will someone who's really fond of dogs—not Mother or S.—look after John please. . . ."

Guy closed the diary and stretched out a hand for his gin and lime. The first swallow was difficult—he was a bit sentimental about dogs himself and he remembered, "Many's the kindness she's done unbeknownst," and he remembered the crisscross lines at the corners of Nancy's eyes and the gray in her hair. And it's true that it is worse to spoil a person's life than to kill someone, and it's true that freedom is a splendid thing. Oh, well, it was no use wasting sympathy on a criminal . . . the gin and lime went down nicely . . . only, once he had thrown a turnip at his brother . . . yes, there, but for the grace of God, went Guy Northeast; there, but for the grace of God, went every one of us.

THE END

Australian train and discovers she could be a murderer in this 1944 novel by the queens of the wacky cozy. Not only does the young woman have a bump on her head and no memory, she also has no idea how she came to be on a train crossing the Nullarbor Plain of Australia with a group of boisterous, argumentative Aussies who appear to be her relatives. Nor does she recall ever having met the young doctor who says he's her fiance. Which is a little awkward, since there's another man on the train who says she'd agreed to marry him, and a love letter in her pocketbook from yet another beau.

She also discovers that she may be a cold-blooded killer. Even worse, she may have really bad taste in clothes, given the outfit she's wearing. When some of her fellow passengers are killed, an Australian cop thinks she would make a great suspect and the only reason she isn't arrested is that the train keeps passing into other jurisdictions. The pasengers also have to keep changing trains, since each Australian state uses a different railroad gauge.

And then there's the matter of the barking lizard in her compartment. The lizard belongs to Uncle Joe, an amateur painter who awakes every morning to discover that someone has defaced his latest masterpiece. It all adds up to some delightful mischief—call it Cornell Woolrich on laughing gas—which is what you would expect from the pens of the two Australian-born Little sisters.

0-915230-22-4 $14.00

The Black Honeymoon
by Constance & Gwenyth Little

Can you murder someone with feathers? If you don't believe that feathers can kill, then you probably haven't read one of the 21 mysteries by the two Little sisters, the reigning queens of the cozy screwball mystery from the 1930s to the 1950s. No, Uncle Richard wasn't tickled to death—though we can't make the same guarantee for readers—but the hyper-allergic rich man did manage to sneeze himself into the hereafter in his hospital room.

Suspicion falls on his nurse, young Miriel Mason, who recently married the dead man's nephew, Ian Ross, an army officer on furlough. Ian managed to sweep Miriel off her feet and to the altar—well, at least to city hall—before she had a chance to check his bank balance, which was nothing to boast about. In fact, Ian cheerfully explains that they'll have to honeymoon in the old family mansion and hope that his relations can leave the two lovebirds alone.

But when Miriel discovers that Ian's motive for marriage may have had nothing to do with her own charms, she decides to postpone at least one aspect of the honeymoon, installing herself and her groom in separate bedrooms. To clear herself of Richard's murder, Miriel summons private detective Kelly, an old crony of her father's, who gets himself hired as a servant in the house even though he can't cook, clean or serve. While Kelly snoops, the body count continues to mount at an alarming rate. Nor is Miriel's hapless father much help. Having squandered the family fortune, he now rents out rooms in his mansion and picks up a little extra cash doing Miriel's laundry.

Originally published in 1944, The Black Honeymoon is filled with tantalizing questions: Who is moaning in the attic? What is the terrible secret in the family

Bible? Why does Aunt Violet insist on staying in her room? Will Kelly get fired for incompetence before he nabs the killer? Will Miriel and Ian ever consummate their marriage? Combining the charm and laughs of a Frank Capra movie with the eccentric characters of a George S. Kaufmann play, *The Black Honeymoon* is a delight from start to finish.   0-915230-21-6 $14.00

The Black Gloves
by Constance & Gwenyth Little

"I'm relishing every madcap moment."—*Murder Most Cozy*

Welcome to the Vickers estate near East Orange, New Jersey, where the middle class is destroying the neighborhood, erecting their horrid little cottages, playing on the Vickers tennis court, and generally disrupting the comfortable life of Hammond Vickers no end.

It's bad enough that he had to shell out good money to get his daughter Lissa a divorce in Reno only to have her brute of an ex-husband show up on his doorstep. But why does there also have to be a corpse in the cellar? And lights going on and off in the attic?

Lissa, on the other hand, welcomes the newcomers into the neighborhood, having spotted a likely candidate for a summer beau among them. But when she hears coal being shoveled in the cellar and finds a blue dandelion near a corpse, what's a girl gonna do but turn detective, popping into people's cottages and dipping dandelions into their inkwells looking for a color match. And she'd better catch the killer fast, because Detective Sergeant Timothy Frobisher says that only a few nail files are standing between her and jail.

Originally published in 1939, *The Black Gloves* was one of 21 wacky mysteries written by the Little sisters and is a sparkling example of the light-hearted cozy mystery that flourished between the Depression and the Korean War. It won't take you long to understand why these long out-of-print titles have so many ardent fans.   0-915230-20-8 $14.00

The Grey Mist Murders
by Constance & Gwenyth Little

Who—or what—is the mysterious figure that emerges from the grey mist to strike down the passengers on the final leg of a round-the-world trip? Is it the same shadowy entity that persists in leaving three matches outside Lady Marsh's cabin every morning? And why does one flimsy negligee seem to pop up at every turn?

When Carla Bray first heard things go bump in the night, she hardly expected to find a corpse in the adjoining cabin. Using up the last of her inheritance, Carla only wanted to have a little innocent fun and perhaps toy with the affections of some of the eligible bachelors on board. However, as the body count mounts, she finds herself the chief suspect in the murders.

Robert Arnold, a sardonic young man who joined the ship in Tahiti, takes an interest in the murders as well as in Carla. But if Robert is really interested in

Carla and wants to help clear her of suspicion, why does he spend so much of his time courting other women on board?

First published in 1938, *The Grey Mist Murders* was the first—and the only book without black in the title—by the two Australian-born Little sisters whose 21 wacky cozies featured independent young women like Carla who weren't averse to marriage—provided no housework was involved.

0-915230-26-7 $14.00

The Rue Morgue Press intends to eventually publish all 21 of the Little mysteries.

Murder, Chop Chop
by James Norman

"The book has the butter-wouldn't-melt-in-his-mouth cool of Rick in *Casablanca*." —*The Rocky Mountain News*. "Amuses the reader no end."—*Mystery News*. "This long out-of-print masterpiece is intricately plotted, full of eccentric characters and very humorous indeed. Highly recommended."—*Mysteries by Mail*

You'll find a cipher or two to crack, a train with a mind of its own, and Chiang Kai-shek's false teeth to cloud the waters in this 1942 classic tale of detection and adventure set during the Sino-Japanese war, with the sleuthing honors going to a gigantic Mexican guerrilla fighter named Gimiendo Quinto and a beautiful Eurasian known as Mountain of Virtue.

0-915230-16-X $13.00

Cook Up a Crime
by Charlotte Murray Russell

"Some wonderful old-time recipes...highly recommended."—*Mysteries by Mail*.

Meet Jane Amanda Edwards, a self-styled "full-fashioned" spinster who complains she hasn't looked at herself in a full-length mirror since Helen Hokinson started drawing for *The New Yorker*. But you can always count on Jane to look into other people's affairs, especially when there's a juicy murder case to investigate. In this 1951 title Jane goes looking for recipes (included between chapters) and finds a body instead. As usual, in one of the longest running jokes in detective fiction, her lily-of-the-field brother Arthur is found clutching the murder weapon.

0-915230-18-6 $13.00

The Man from Tibet
by Clyde B. Clason

"The novels of American classicist Clason have been unavailable for years, a lapse happily remedied with the handsome trade paperback reprint of (Westborough's) best known case. Clason spun ornate puzzles in the manner of Carr and Queen and spread erudition as determinedly as Van Dine."—Jon L. Breen, *Ellery Queen's Mystery Magazine*. "A highly original and practical locked-room murder method."— Robert C.S. Adey.

The elderly historian, Professor Theocritus Lucius Westborough, solves a cozy 1938 locked room mystery involving a Tibetan lama in Chicago in which the murder weapon may well be an eighth century manuscript. The result is a fair-play puzzler for fans of John Dickson Carr. With an extensive bibliography, it is also one of the first popular novels to examine in depth then-forbidden Tibet and Tibetan Buddhism.

0-915230-17-8 $14.00

Murder is a Collector's Item
by Elizabeth Dean

"Completely enjoyable."—*New York Times.* "Fast and funny."—*The New Yorker.* *"Murder is a Collector's Item* froths over with the same effervescent humor as the best Hepburn-Grant films."— Sujata Massey, Agatha-award-winning author of *The Salaryman's Wife* and *Zen Attitude.*

Twenty-six-year-old Emma Marsh isn't much at spelling or geography and perhaps she butchers the odd literary quotation or two, but she's a keen judge of character and more than able to hold her own when it comes to selling antiques or solving murders. When she stumbles upon the body of a rich collector on the floor of the Boston antiques shop where she works, suspicion quickly falls upon her missing boss. Emma knows Jeff Graham is no murderer, but veteran homicide cop Jerry Donovan doesn't share her conviction.

With a little help from Hank Fairbanks, her wealthy boyfriend and would-be criminologist, Emma turns sleuth and cracks the case, but not before a host of cops, reporters and customers drift through the shop on Charles Street, trading insults and sipping scotch as they talk clues, prompting a *New York Times* reviewer to remark that Emma "drinks far more than a nice girl should."

Emma does a lot of things that women didn't do in detective novels of the 1930s. In an age of menopausal spinsters, deadly sirens, admiring wives and air-headed girlfriends, pretty, big-footed Emma Marsh stands out. She's a precursor of the independent women sleuths that finally came into their own in the last two decades of this century.

Originally published in 1939, *Murder is a Collector's Item* was the first of three books featuring Emma. Smoothly written and sparkling with dry, sophisticated humor, it combines an intriguing puzzle with an entertaining portrait of a self-possessed young woman on her own in Boston toward the end of the Great Depression. Author Dean, who worked in a Boston antiques shop, offers up an insider's view of what that easily impressed *Times* reviewer called the "goofy" world of antiques. Lovejoy, the rogue antiques dealer in Jonathan Gash's mysteries, would have loved Emma.

0-915230-19-4 $14.00

The Mirror
by Marlys Millhiser

"Completely enjoyable."—*Library Journal*."A great deal of fun."—*Publishers Weekly*.

How could you not be intrigued, as one reviewer pointed out, by a novel in which "you find the main character marrying her own grandfather and giving birth to her own mother?" Such is the situation in Marlys Millhiser's classic novel (a Mystery Guild selection originally published by Putnam in 1978) of two women who end up living each other's lives after they look into an antique Chinese mirror.

Twenty-year-old Shay Garrett is not aware that she's pregnant and is having second thoughts about marrying Marek Weir when she's suddenly transported back 78 years in time into the body of Brandy McCabe, her own grandmother, who is unwillingly about to be married off to miner Corbin Strock. Shay's in shock but she still recognizes that the picture of her grandfather that hangs in the family home doesn't resemble her husband-to-be. But marry Corbin she does and off she goes to the high mining town of Nederland, where this thoroughly modern young woman has to learn to cope with such things as wood cooking stoves and—to her—old-fashioned attitudes about sex. Shay's ability to see into the future has her mother-in-law thinking she's a witch and others calling her a psychic but Shay was an indifferent student at best and not all of her predictions hit the mark: remember that "day of infamy" when the Japanese attacked Pearl Harbor—Dec. *11*, 1941?

In the meantime, Brandy McCabe is finding it even harder to cope with life in the Boulder, Colorado, of 1978. After all, her wedding is about to be postponed due to her own death—at least the death of her former body—at the age of 98. And, in spite of the fact she's a virgin, she's about to give birth. And *this* young woman does have some very old-fashioned ideas about sex, which leaves her husband-to-be—and father of her child—very puzzled. *The Mirror* is even more of a treat for today's readers, given that it is now a double trip back in time. Not only can readers look back on life at the turn of the century, they can also revisit the days of disco and the sexual revolution of the 1970's.

So how does one categorize *The Mirror?* Is it science fiction? Fantasy? Supernatural? Mystery? Romance? Historical fiction? You'll find elements of each but in the end it's a book driven by that most magical of all literary devices: imagine if... .

0-915230-15-1 $14.95

About The Rue Morgue Press

The Rue Morgue Press Classic Mystery line is designed to bring back into print those books that were favorites of readers between the turn of the century and 1960. The editors welcome suggestions for reprints. To receive our catalog or to make suggestions, write The Rue Morgue Press, P.O. Box 4119, Boulder, Colorado 80306.